MASTER OF SECRETS

SIENNA SNOW

GODS OF VEGAS, BOOK 4

By Sienna Snow

Copyright Page

DEDICATION

I dedicate Master of Secrets to my friend and keeper Catherine Anderson. She cheers me on, kicks me in the ass, and tells me which way is up. She knows what to say and exactly when to say it.

Finishing this book was harder and more emotional than anything I had written to date. It forced me to explore a dark world no one should ever experience. Without Catherine's encouragement and pushiness, I would never have finished writing this book or survived the editing process.

Catherine - Thank you for jumping on my crazy train. I cherish your friendship more than you could ever know.

CHAPTER ONE

Anaya

"You know the drill. Don't get distracted and check in exactly at twenty-three hundred." My handler Briana's Italian-accented demand rang into my earpiece.

"Copy." I stared at my image in the antique wood-framed mirror, touching up the last of my makeup.

I had one job to do. Find a way into the Trevolo Mansion located in the heart of Venice, avoid arousing suspicion, plant the trackers, and leave without getting caught. As long as the recon was accurate, the job would be a piece of cake.

Tonight, I wasn't Anaya Anthony, the product of an illicit affair between international criminal Victor Anthony and Greek socialite Rhea Lykaios. Instead, I was a trained and honed Solon agent on a mission.

This wasn't my first undercover operation, but it was my most high profile and first as the lead. My usual assignments involved behind-the-scenes monitoring and targeting where interacting with anyone was considered a hazard to my job. This time, I was out in public, with an assumed name and a fabricated background so rock solid that my family wouldn't be able to find me.

"Coast is clear. Head downstairs. Going dark for sixty, starting now." Briana disconnected, leaving me to my task. I'd meet up with her near the pool house in precisely an hour.

I checked my reflection one last time. I adjusted my blond hair so it looked a little unkempt, in the style of my persona. One day I'd go back to my natural color, a rich black-brown. At least it was still long and Briana hadn't advised me to cut it.

Smoothing down my cap-sleeve Monica Malone gown, I opened the door to the bathroom and made my way through the hallway that led to the ballroom.

A security guard smiled in my direction and then gave me a head-to-toe survey. I'd noticed him checking me out earlier, and it looked like he hadn't lost interest. He was one of three men patrolling the area around the residence.

"Excuse me," I said to him in Italian. *"Do you know what time dinner is expected to start?"*

He glanced at his watch. *"Not for another hour."*

I sighed and then covered my stomach. *"I should have had a snack to hold me over. But then again, I'm not sure Mrs. Trevolo would have let me take a break with all the craziness of the party."*

The guard's face lit up as if he'd discovered something. *"Now I know where I've seen you. You're Anastasia Ashton, Monica Malone's assistant. You helped design all Mrs. Trevolo's gowns for tonight's event."*

I made a show of wincing. *"Guilty as charged."*

As far as the world knew, I was the eccentric world-renowned designer's assistant. I worked as the go-to between client and fashion icon, always in the background, never taking attention from the "boss." In reality, Monica worked for me, playing the high-maintenance persona for my cover. I looked, dressed, and acted like a nerdy, super-conservative, mousy assistant. Nothing like my real-life, high-fashion persona of Anaya Anthony, baby sister to the international business moguls known as the Lykaios brothers.

"I heard Mrs. T was giving you trouble."

The Trevolos were notorious for their over-the-top antics when it came to events. And Mrs. T, as the guard called her, wasn't happy her gown was too snug for her to breathe. I'd warned her that after a baby it was better to go up in size, but she'd insisted she'd return to her pre-baby figure within a few weeks post delivery. Since I'd never had a child, I hadn't argued too much, but the drama I'd dealt with earlier in the day made me wish I had. Then again, she was part of the notorious underworld duo who specialized in human assets for various purposes, many of which would turn anyone's stomach.

"You could say that." I wrung my hands together, trying to shy away from discussing my client. *"It's just part of the job."*

"I hear you. The Trevolos are demanding but pay well."

"That is true. You wouldn't happen to know where I could grab a snack, maybe some crackers? I just need something to hold me over."

"I can do better. Come this way." He gestured to his left. *"Chef has a spread for the staff hidden in the butler's pantry. Since Mrs. T is busy mingling, you won't have to worry about any wardrobe malfunctions."*

"You're a godsend," I squealed with a bit more enthusiasm than I should have, playing into my awkward cover personality.

I let the guard direct me through the kitchen, past the back stairwell leading to the family wing, and toward the butler's room.

"Feel free to eat your fill. You never know when you'll get your next meal, especially if Mrs. T goes into full meltdown."

"Thank you," I whispered and grabbed a handful of almonds.

"Enjoy. Hopefully I'll see you soon." He inclined his head and left me to continue his duties.

I lingered for a few minutes, nibbling on nuts and cheese. The butler's area was better than the kitchens of some of the best restaurants in the world. High-shine steel cabinets and counters displayed the various food choices as if arranged for a photoshoot.

The Trevolos definitely knew how to build a house. Too bad their moral code was worse than the lowest scum of the earth. It had taken six months of investigating to get this far into their world. We had a contact on the inside of their operation who periodically fed us information, but I knew, as did my superiors, that unless I became one of the victims of their crimes, I'd never get truly close enough to take them down.

The world believed they were perfect, and they kept up that image to a T.

Once I'd wasted enough time, I casually made my way around the corner and up the back stairwell, strategically angling myself out of the security camera's line of sight. From the blueprints I'd studied earlier in the day, I knew the server room was on the far right corner of the residential side of the second story.

I slipped off my heels just as I reached the wooden floor landing and tiptoed barefoot to my targeted room.

The sounds of laughter echoed down the hall, and I quickly slipped into the room.

"Fucking hell," I murmured to myself. This wasn't a server room for a house; it was the type found in the top tech companies around the world. The only reason the Trevolos would need something like this was to cover their tracks. This was always the way it was—those who publicly prided themselves for their philanthropy and charities were the ones involved in the most disgusting aspects of life.

My stomach knotted. This assignment was way bigger than any of us had anticipated. My gut said I needed to get the hell out of the mansion as soon as I finished my task.

Lifting the hem of my dress, I pulled off the tracers attached to my garter. It took me a little under three minutes to place the remote devices.

Taking a deep breath, I went to the door, cracked it a fraction, and took a look. Once I met up with Briana, I'd have to mentally and physically prepare for my "abduction."

God only knew what I'd end up having to do to achieve my goal. I had to keep reminding myself it was worth it if I saved a single life.

Just as I moved to step outside, a hand grabbed me and shoved me against the wall.

"Not so fast, Ms. Anthony. I think it's time we had a little conversation."

My heart hammered into my head as I stared into a pair of angry emerald eyes that had haunted me for more nights than I wanted to admit. They were the irises of the man who'd broken the heart of the innocent girl I'd been and made me hate him to the point I had avoided any contact with him for over five years.

"Looks like I caught a little dove snooping in places she shouldn't."

I ignored his use of the pet name he'd given me when he'd discovered the dove tattoo I'd gotten on a trip to Bora Bora with my sister.

"Ia...Adrian. What the hell are you doing here?"

His grip tightened on my arm, and his six-foot-three, muscled body leaned closer to mine. "I should be the one asking you the same question, but I already know the answer."

"I have no idea what you're talking about. I got lost. I thought this was the direction of Mrs. Trevolo's dressing suite. I'm here to make sure everything is perfect for her."

"Ana. Do not lie to me." His words were laced with authority and irritation.

I narrowed my gaze. "I'm not. Check with the staff. I've spent the day putting out wardrobe fires."

One of Adrian's large hands moved to my throat. A prickle of awareness and arousal hit me as it had in the past when he'd touched me.

His pupils dilated, telling me he felt it too.

"Who do you work for?"

I couldn't hide the surprise on my face. "Monica Malone."

"Let me repeat. Who do you work for?"

"I think you're delusional. I'm a marketing and design geek, remember? How do you think Penny gets all those designer gowns?"

Penny was my first cousin through our mothers and Adrian's half sister on their father's side. Penny was also married to my half brother. Our relationships were a sordid tangled mess, filled with so many scandals that it would boggle the mind. We were very Greek, as my half sister Henna liked to tell me.

Adrian gave a slight squeeze to my throat. "Ana, I'm going to ask you one more time, and if you lie to me, I'm going to throw you over my shoulder and carry you out of here and toss you on the next plane back to Las Vegas so your family can sort this out."

I gave him a calculated grin. "I'd like to see you try."

Adrian had no idea who he was dealing with. I'd laid men bigger than him on their ass. It was the first thing I'd learned in training. Let my opponent think he or she had the advantage. I wasn't petite like my sister and Penny, but neither was I tall. I was an average five foot six.

"Your training isn't going to work on me. I've been in the game longer than you."

His words made my heartbeat accelerate. I stared into his eyes and realized I was in so much trouble.

"Who do *you* work for, Adrian? I've always known your computer-nerd, hacker persona was a cover for the other things you were into. No one can gather the type of data you seem to procure without government clearance."

"Ian. Say it, Ana. That's what you've called me since we were children."

I narrowed my gaze. "I asked you a question, *Adrian*."

"Stubborn," he muttered under his breath before he said, "A cybersecurity expert the Trevolos hired to make sure only invited guests made it onto their property. Imagine my surprise when the facial recognition software labeled a woman whose face I'd recognize in any crowd, even with blond hair, as Anastasia Ashton, the lowly, hyper-shy assistant to Monica Malone instead of Anaya Anthony, the woman I've known since she was in diapers."

"Now who's lying?"

"Is this a game of tit for tat?"

I shoved at his chest, using a defensive move I'd practiced less than a few hours before and sending him back for a second. But he shifted too fast and had me pinned against the door with my arms above my head and his very aroused body pressed to the front of mine.

He felt so good against me, reminding me of things I had worked too hard to forget.

Damn him for making me want him.

Hell, who was I kidding? I never stopped wanting him.

He *tsked*. "First rule of training is to never let your guard down, even if you know your assailant."

"I hate you," I hissed through gritted teeth. "You're definitely CIA. They're always too cocky for their own good. I bet you fit right in."

He didn't deny my assessment. Instead he said, "And you're Solon."

I snorted. "Like in the Greek philosopher? I think you've lost your mind."

"No." He glared down at me. "I'm referring to the underground vigilante organization that regularly ignores international law in order to achieve its goals. The organization known for recruiting college students, training them to become human weapons, and sending them into situations that put them at risk for being kidnapped, if not killed."

I remained quiet. Nothing I could say would change his belief.

God, how long had he known? Why hadn't he ratted me out to my family? My career couldn't end like this. I'd finally made it to lead. All I needed was another few years and I'd happily go back to Las Vegas and take over some of my family's businesses.

I had to figure out a way to get Adrian to keep his mouth shut.

"Nothing to say, Ms. Anthony? I will blow your cover

if you don't stop. I refuse to be the one to tell your family that something happened to you."

The determination on his face told me he would do exactly what he said. And that would bring a whole load of issues I wasn't ready to deal with. My brothers, not to mention my sister, were overprotective on a good day. If they even had an inclination of what I was doing as my "real" job, they'd have me quarantined to Vegas with around-the-clock guards. It wouldn't matter that I was twenty-six years old. To them I was the baby, a child to be protected from the scandal of my illegitimate birth.

"And what about you? Do my brothers know you're CIA?"

His lips curved. "As a matter of fact, they do. As does your sister. It helps them out on occasion, especially when it comes to vetting their business partners."

"Dammit, Adrian, I won't let you take my career from me. I've worked too long and hard."

"And I won't let you come home in a body bag."

"Then let me finish my assignment. The longer you keep me in here, the more likely I'll get caught."

"I'm not stupid enough to think you're going to actually become the marketing and social media expert you have your family believing you are."

"I won't apologize for what I do. Because of people like me, lives of countless women and children are saved."

"I can say the same for myself, but unlike you, when I

break the law, it's approved by my government and won't cause an international incident."

This was the argument Solon agents had dealt with since the inception of the organization. Solon had no loyalty to any country and was funded privately through various donors throughout the world. It was run like a government security agency without the bureaucracy. Unlike what Adrian probably believed, Solon would go to hell and back to protect its agents. There was always a contingency plan.

And mine was about to get activated if I didn't leave this room soon and report in.

Plus, I had to prepare for my meeting with my contact in Trevolo's underground. He was arranging my "abduction" and transportation to one of Trevolo's pleasure islands designed as playgrounds for the rich, privileged, and most dirty of the world, where Trevolo housed his harems and threw lavish parties designed around every sexual fantasy.

The women who serviced the men were there by their own choice, preferring a life carefree of responsibility in exchange for the use of their bodies. From what I'd learned, they were treated for the most part like pampered princesses. It was the hidden aspect of the place that I wanted to infiltrate. A place the majority of those who visited the island had no clue even existed.

Only those in Trevolo's inner circle knew his real

business: the sale of women and children, ripped from their lives and then placed in underground auctions.

"We're getting nowhere. I have to finish my assignment. What do you want from me so I can get out of here?"

A crease formed between Adrian's brows. "What are you offering me?"

I clenched my jaw. He wasn't going to make this easy. Nothing with this man was easy.

"Whatever you want, as long as you keep your mouth shut. If my family hears one word of this, the deal is off."

"Anything I want?" He leaned his face closer to mine, and immediately I felt a shiver shoot down my spine.

I licked my lips. "Yes. You're the master of secrets, what's one more to the pile?"

"Well then, I want what I said we couldn't have five years ago."

"You can't be serious. We live on different continents. Besides, you're the one who thought I was too innocent for the things you wanted."

"You said anything, Ana."

"Dammit, Adrian. I will not marry you again. One drunken mistake was enough."

"If I recall, neither of us was drunk."

No, I was just stupid enough to believe you loved me as much as I loved you.

"It makes no difference. I wasn't the one who got cold feet or wanted an annulment."

A flash of something passed in his gaze and then was quickly masked. "Dammit, Ana. I was twenty-two years old and you were barely twenty-one."

"And your point is?" I lifted my chin.

"I didn't want to hold you back. You'd just finished your internship and gotten your dream job. If only I'd known what it really was, then I may have insisted we stayed married even if you hated me in the long run."

"I don't want to go there." I clenched my teeth. "Just tell me what you want. I'll accept anything as long as it doesn't involve marrying you."

"Are you sure you want to strike that kind of bargain?"

"Adrian," I warned.

"What if I said I want you back in my bed?"

My pulse jumped.

"Why would you want that? Remember, I'm too innocent to handle what you want."

"You aren't the same woman from five years ago." He rubbed his hard cock against my aching clit. "And I'm definitely not the same man."

He bit my lower lip and it nearly took all my strength not to moan.

"Not possible," I said through a breathless whisper.

"And why is that?"

"Because I'm on assignment. I won't have time for

you."

"Oh, Ana, you have no idea. You will have plenty of time for me."

I frowned. "What the fuck does that mean?"

"You see, I have a meeting with a certain Anastasia Ashton tomorrow. I'm supposed to capture her." His voice grew angrier than before. "And give her to a distributor who was planning on selling her on the black market through one of Trevolo's auctions."

Oh fuck.

I'd known from the beginning I was working with a CIA operative who'd established a base in Trevolo's world, but I never suspected it was...

"Nothing to say?"

"You're my man on the inside?"

"Yes."

"How long have you known it was me?"

He stepped away from me and ran a frustrated hand through his perfectly groomed hair. "Not until I saw you on the security feed a month ago."

"This is why you haven't been home in the last year."

"How would you know? The last time you went home was two years ago."

I wanted to argue but then kept my mouth shut. In my attempt to avoid Adrian, I'd all but isolated myself from my family.

"That's not important right now. What I want to know

is if you're going to let me finish my assignment or fuck it up for me."

"Do you mean, am I going to give you to a smuggler, buy you in an illegal auction, and then fuck you?"

My breath hitched. I'd avoided thinking about the latter part of his question for months. I'd known what was expected of me. I was going to be one of the women on one of Trevolo's islands, expected to service the master who bought me for the weeks I was there.

Since I would be a "special jewel," a woman who'd been "kidnapped" and sold as part of Trevolo's sex trafficking ring, I'd leave the island with my purchaser. I'd convinced myself it would be easier to have sex with a stranger for the assignment, keeping it business, rather than being with a man who I was emotionally tied to, who could tear my heart to shreds, who I loved.

Well, that was all shot to hell.

Wait a second, he had been intending to fuck someone for the job too.

"Why are you so upset at the prospect of sleeping with me? The only difference now is that you know the woman you're going to partner with. We can both make the sacrifices."

Anger burned in his eyes. "You would rather fuck a complete stranger than me?"

"A complete stranger didn't reject me and then leave me without knowing what happened between us." I closed my eyes, squeezing them tight, and tried my best to rein in my emotions.

"Dammit, Ana, it wasn't like that."

"I don't want to talk about it." I lifted a hand. "We will go the way it was planned. You will sell me, buy me, and then fuck me. We will play our roles, finish the assignment, but that's where it will end. What we had is gone. When this is over, we go our separate ways."

I had to make myself believe the words I'd just spoken were possible. I knew getting involved with him again would guarantee another broken heart.

Work had been the escape from the pain of what happened between us, and now my work was the reason he was back in my life.

Adrian moved forward until he had my back pressed against the wall again. "Ana, it has never been and never will be as cold as you're trying to make it. Sex was the one place we never, ever had any issues. We've done everything and anything a couple can do together. I know your body better than you do."

He was always so fucking cocky.

"Then I guess we're in agreement. Since we've previously done everything, it shouldn't be so hard to keep it business."

"You are so fucking stubborn." He tilted my chin up. "Your reaction to me from just a few moments ago tells me business is the last thing that it will ever be between us."

"I won't let you hurt me again." Dammit, I was not supposed to let him see the pain I'd never gotten over.

With everyone else, I could keep my composure, but this man turned me into an emotional mess.

"The last thing I want to do is hurt you."

He leaned down and kissed my lips, in the feather-soft way he'd done when we were in college, in the way that always made me give in. "In fact, I was working on a plan to get you back."

His words brought me back to reality, and I pushed him away. "Yes, I believe that. Especially when you were going to fuck your Solon associate for this assignment."

How many women had he fucked for the job? Yes, I knew I was planning to do the same damn thing, but I never expected to get back with my ex. I'd chosen a line of work that would keep me from any relationship and had accepted it.

I glanced at my watch. Fuck, I had to check in. Briana would lose her shit if I didn't make contact soon.

"I have to go or there won't be an assignment." I turned, shifting behind him and moved to the door.

Adrian blocked my way. "We aren't done here."

"Yes, we are. You'll get my body and cooperation for the assignment. I'll even let you lead since you know the rules of the inside. But you'll never have anything else. Ana and Ian died the day you filed for the annulment."

CHAPTER TWO

Adrian

As soon as the door shut after Ana left the server room, I gripped the back of my neck and shook my head.

What the hell was she thinking accepting this assignment? She was going to use her body to get the job done. It fucking infuriated me to think she'd let some fucker I worked with touch her.

I knew this damn Solon/Interpol/CIA project would end up biting me in the ass. I never expected it to involve the one woman who meant more to me than anyone else on earth.

This was not how I'd planned to get her back. Five

years—I'd waited five damn years, only to have it fucked up here.

There was no way I could convince her I was sincere about wanting her back.

What woman would believe the job was a job and everything I'd done was only because I had to convince Trevolo and his circle I was one of them?

I'd hate the idea of Ana fucking a man because it was part of her job. Hell, that was what she was about to do.

Was the universe telling me I was screwed beyond repair?

I'd hurt Ana the first time to keep her from giving up her dreams for me. Now I was going to hurt her for the second time by making her into my whore.

I wasn't going to lie and say I didn't want her in my bed, but I'd planned to seduce her, get her to fall in love with me again, get her to forgive me for being such a shithead.

Well, that plan was down the toilet.

I pulled out my phone as it beeped to find a message from Trevolo. He wanted data on a few potential art clients. Which I knew was code for buyers of his "special jewels" as he liked to call them. Trevolo had a thing about calling those he auctioned jewels. The "harem jewels" were the women who came to his private islands around the world of their own accord. They traded their bodies for a life of luxury where every expense was paid for. This was a stark contrast to his "special jewels," the women and children stolen from their lives and sold on the black market for God knew what.

I'd spent the last two years posing undercover as the son of a well-known arms dealer, the boogeyman of the European underworld that no one knew was a fictitious creation on the part of the CIA and Interpol. My job was to infiltrate Trevolo's organization and find out who the buyers for the "special jewels" were. He was my middleman for the sale of my military goods, and for his services, I'd worked cybersecurity for his various properties and businesses and supported his auctions by purchasing his "harem jewels."

I'd placed Anastasia Ashton in the pool of special jewels through a third party, before I'd known who she really was. Her background and dedication matched what we needed for the assignment. I'd always had my reservations about working with Solon because they were known for going rogue, but I accepted I had no say in what the higher-ups decided.

As instructed by my director, I'd arranged for Anastasia's abduction and placement in the special auction. All of it would take place on Trevolo's private island in the Virgin Islands. I'd had an official invitation to participate in the special auction for months, with the time and date to be determined.

It was the perfect setup to get into the area of the

island that wasn't part of Trevolo's public harem, an area where women and children were sold as real slaves and weren't on the island by choice.

Now the thought of Ana being part of this world not only pissed me the fuck off but made my stomach hurt.

It was hard to keep in mind that we were working to end an evil aspect of humanity when the bait was the one I viewed as mine.

I shot Trevolo a quick response and then messaged my team. I scanned the room to see what Anaya had attached to the various modules. It took me a few seconds, but I found all eight of her trackers. I left them in place and held in an oath.

This little stunt was not part of the fucking plan. The woman was playing with people who would sell her to the most disgusting fucker on the planet, or kill her outright, if she were ever to get caught. That was after they raped her repeatedly.

Of all the women in the world to end up on assignment with, it had to be Anaya Anthony. I'd left her to keep her safe and instead she'd spent the last five years doing God knew what.

I'd nearly gone out of my mind the second I'd spotted her on Trevolo's security feed. All these years, she'd avoided me, finding every excuse to be away whenever I was visiting my sister, even going as far as missing Penny's baby shower a few months ago. Then through some twist of fate, she popped up in the one place I never expected, in the middle of my fucking assignment as my fucking contact.

No matter what her name was on paper, or how she'd changed her hair color or style, no one on earth could make me believe she wasn't the girl I'd loved since I was barely a teenager.

When I'd investigated her cover, I found it was tighter than any of the ones I'd encountered in all the years I'd worked as a cybersecurity expert for the CIA. Her history had everything from report cards and health records to family pictures. According to the persona created for her, she was a New York City-raised, middle-class, overachieving daughter of a commercial truck mechanic and a homemaker. She'd attended design school on a scholarship and then began interning for Monica Malone, who'd hired her on full time last year. To anyone who looked her up, they would only find Anastasia Ashton.

Ana's relationship with socialite Briana Amici should have tipped me off that she worked for Solon. Briana, in addition to being my sister Penny's close friend, was a trainer and handler for the rogue agency. It wouldn't have surprised me if she was the one who'd recruited Anaya.

I checked my watch and noted fifteen minutes had passed since Ana left.

I exited the server room, taking an extra few seconds to

lock the door, and made my way to the ballroom, where the gala was in full swing.

God, I hated these things. I'd been to more than my share of them during my youth. My mother, Dara Kipos, had insisted I live up to my responsibility as the heir to Kipos International, a horticultural conglomerate that she'd all but stolen out from under Penny's feet. Thankfully, those days were over. Today my mother lived in a halfway house in a remote town in Montana after serving seven years for fraud.

How insane was it that two children of criminals had become agents of organizations that fought crime? Although the one I was part of was sanctioned by a recognized government and not illegal.

I was a fucking hypocrite. I'd overlooked the shit Trevolo was into for over a year and a half in order to get deeper into his world.

But the thought of anything happening to Ana was unbearable. There was no way of getting her out of this assignment without blowing my cover or years of work.

Fuck, I was going to have to let my Interpol partner, Sebastian, know Ana was here. He'd been my friend since college and had been an eyewitness to the mess that had become my relationship with Ana. I hadn't told him I knew the true identity of Anastasia Ashton. When he found out, he'd be pissed.

She was my weakness and he knew it.

After he got over his irritation with me, he'd probably tell me I deserved to see her like this for being such a hardass about working with Solon.

Scanning the room, I found Sebastian charming one of Trevolo's nieces. Sebastian had no need for a cover—he was the son of Jonas Weber, international financier and head of an underground German crime syndicate. He posed as the heir apparent to the empire but worked with Interpol as a fuck-you to his father for his hard stance on negotiating with enemies. Jonas Weber had all but told his rival to kill his wife when she was kidnapped and refused to consider paying the ransom for her safe return. Sebastian's mother had washed up on the shores of the Spree River in Berlin with her neck slit.

I never probed the crazy dynamics of Sebastian's loyalties, especially since mine weren't any less fucked up.

Sebastian caught me glancing at him, lifted a brow, and gave me a signal that we needed to talk. He pulled out his phone and typed something. A second later, my mobile buzzed.

Saw your dove. You've been holding out, old man. Is this an extraction situation?

I wish, I responded. *She's my contact.*

This is about to become interesting. Hope she doesn't shoot you in your sleep.

The fact he didn't seem surprised by my news gave me

the distinct impression he'd known Ana was our Solon agent.

It seems I'm not the only one holding out. I wanted to wipe that grin from the cocky bastard's face.

It was a need-to-know situation.

I typed *Asshole* and then slipped my phone back in my pocket.

I strolled the periphery of the ballroom until I found Ana attending to Catarina Trevolo. Mrs. T was a bitch on a normal day, and on gala days, she was an all-out evil queen. There was an annoyed crease between Ana's brows, but she nodded and listened to whatever Catarina was complaining about.

I picked up a glass of champagne, took a sip, and watched a group of men glance in Ana's direction. No matter how hard she tried, she couldn't play down her beauty. Ana stood out even in her too-big-for-her-body, nondescript dress one would find adorning a ninety-year-old matron.

She had the high cheekbones and almond eyes of her birth mother and the golden tanned skin of her Indian father. And those eyes—I could still remember the countless nights I'd spent staring into those golden amber eyes. Never had I seen another human being with irises in that shade. I would have believed they were artificial if I hadn't seen them cloud with both passion and anger.

Catarina must have noticed the attention Ana was

getting and frowned, grabbing her by the upper arm and leading her to a side room.

Jealous bitch.

I wasted another twenty minutes in the ballroom before I slipped out the back of the mansion and strolled toward the boathouse the Trevolos had given me as my base of operations.

Something crunched under my foot, causing me to pause.

I stooped down and felt a lump form in the pit of my stomach. It was one of Ana's earrings. Reaching around my tuxedo jacket and toward the back of my pants, I pulled out my pistol. Moving as quietly as possible, I went in the direction of the docks.

When I got there, I found Ana's shoes scattered in different spots, as if they were dropped in a struggle, and the usual boat docked on the pier was gone.

CHAPTER THREE

Adrian

I stepped out of my jet and onto the private airstrip on a remote island nestled between the British and Dutch Virgin Islands.

Adjusting my jacket, I waited for Spencer, the island's manager, to approach me.

Trevolo enjoyed a lot of pomp and circumstance, which meant I'd have to play my role to a T in order to get Ana back. From this moment on, I was Julian Bonaparte, hacker, drug lord, and all-around scum of the earth.

It had taken Sebastian calling in backup to keep me from taking apart the Trevolos' Italian mansion after I'd realized Ana had been taken. Then I'd had to deal with

Briana Amici and her Solon crew, who were pissed to holy hell and blaming me for compromising Ana.

If things had gone according to plan, we'd have known her exact whereabouts, but because of the unplanned abduction, we'd been at a loss. There were at least four auctions taking place at any given time and at varying locations across the world. The only place that was consistent was Catarina Island, Trevolo's personal sex retreat. The sick bastard had named the place after his wife.

It took a month of working in conjunction with Solon and Interpol to find out the location of where Ana was taken. And that was only the result of a communication on the dark web alluding to an amber-eyed prize available for purchase as one of Trevolo's special jewels.

I'd known without a doubt that they were talking about Ana. Those fucking eyes of hers were beyond unique. What I couldn't figure out was why they'd taken her in the first place.

Then a few days ago, around the time Solon was going to send in a team to extract Ana, I received a notice that it was time to visit the island for two weeks of "relaxation and pleasure."

After quite a bit of convincing, we were able to persuade the higher-ups at Solon to stand down for two more weeks. If they went nuts, years of work would go down the toilet. My job was to proceed as previously planned.

Find out the exact date of the special auction, and who the key buyers were, bid on Ana, use her as my slave, and get the fuck out of the way when the agencies descended on Trevolo.

"Mr. Bonaparte, we are honored to have you join us. Your bungalow is ready, per your instructions." Spencer's English had a touch of the Caribbean.

He was native to the area, but from a different island. Most of the staff only came in for the days and left in the evenings. Trevolo only kept a loyal group of servants around at all times.

I gave a nod but said nothing. I kept a bungalow on the outskirts of the island. It was a courtesy Trevolo gave me only because of my fictitious father and the power he wielded. In truth, the bastard hated me.

I was an asshole and he was one right back. We essentially played a game of chess with each other, seeing how far we could push before the other gave in or came back harder. It was a fucked-up way to play power games, but that was the way it worked.

"If you'll follow me. Mr. Trevolo is waiting for you on the terrace with the other guests."

Spencer led me to a waiting Jeep and after a short drive, we arrived at a palatial white stone and stucco mansion overlooking the ocean. If I hadn't known what happened inside its walls, I'd consider this the perfect island paradise.

Trevolo used the island as a place to win favor with his business associates.

He would provide access to his harem jewels through his harem auction and then each of the highest bidders would have a personal slave of his choosing to see to every one of his needs. The only rules were that those women were never abused to the point of needing medical attention and they stayed on the island when the guests left.

The few women who left the island were the ones who came with the guests as their kept slaves and those purchased in the special auctions.

Until now, I'd only participated in the auctions for his harem jewels. The open-ended invitation he'd given me had me and my superiors suspicious. Trevolo wanted something from Julian Bonaparte.

Still, I was thankful for that invitation because I knew Ana would be one of the women in the special auction.

I would pay anything to get her back, including using my own personal fortune.

I walked into the grand entryway and was immediately greeted by a uniformed guard. He scanned me from head to toe then let me pass.

"Ahh, the elusive Julian Bonaparte has arrived." Trevolo greeted me. "You left so abruptly during the party

I thought something was wrong. But then again, you are the troubleshooter for your family. When duty calls, one must go."

"As you said, duty comes first." I shook his hand and let him lead me toward his other guests.

"I'm glad you adjusted your plans to visit the island."

"You did insist there is a unique selection that I shouldn't miss."

"One in particular seemed just your taste. She reminded me the type of harem jewels you enjoy taking to bed during our pleasure weekends, so I set her aside for you."

Well, fuck. I hadn't realized I'd gravitated toward women who reminded me of Ana until now. My preoccupation with Ana was the only reason for this fucking mess.

"Who is she?"

"She is someone perfect for you. She's a fighter. She needs a strong hand and a firm will. When we discovered her fiery spirit, I was even more positive that I had to offer her to you first."

What the hell had they done to Anaya over the last month? Anger pulsed at the base of my neck.

Keep it together, asshole. Play the part.

I'd concocted a reputation for liking rough, pushing-the-limits sex. On occasion going as far as engaging in some hardcore kink to keep the image alive. And now I had to live it, even if it meant fucking Anaya in front of everyone on the island.

The fact I was aroused by the idea of marking Ana as mine made me one sick bastard.

"So no other special prizes are going up today?"

"Just the one. The rest of my special items will arrive at a later date. And their bidding is only open to a few. You're more than welcome to purchase more than one prize, but I'm positive the one I've selected for you will keep you occupied."

"I find it hard to believe I am the only one you are offering her to. There are others who have similar preferences."

A slight calculating gleam entered Trevolo's eyes. "For the right price, she is yours."

"You haven't answered my question." I held his gaze.

"There was one other who would see her value, but he is delayed."

Well, thank God for small favors.

"You know as I do, I can outbid anyone on this island."

"Yes. That is true. However, the gentleman in question isn't here to challenge. Only you and I know what I am offering you."

It couldn't be this easy. Trevolo was up to something.

"What's the catch?"

"You know me well, friend." Trevolo gestured to a small alcove away from some of the guests who were moving about the terrace. "I need your father's assistance with a shipment out of Indonesia."

"I'm listening." I casually slid a hand into my pocket, activating a recorder that couldn't be detected. This would add to evidence we were collecting to bring down Trevolo.

Trevolo was a slippery motherfucker, who'd found ways of keeping his hands clean and the Italian authorities out of his business. Buying Ana and the recording wouldn't be enough to bring Trevolo down. I needed the actual list of buyers and the time and date the human cargo would arrive for the auction.

"In exchange for me giving you the exclusive opportunity to purchase this special jewel, you will speak with your father about accepting a shipment onto your cargo barges and bringing it to your port in Cyprus."

He knew as well as I did that I "ran" the empire. His respect toward "my father" was a formality.

Trevolo was running drugs into Europe and needed the transport.

"Who will collect the cargo?"

"Our normal carriers will pick it up."

"Let me be clear. For our cooperation, I gain your prized jewel."

"Well, for the correct price."

"I'm not sure a woman is worth the trouble."

A frown marred Trevolo's face before he schooled it away. "Let me offer this in addition. I will let you keep half of my shipment in addition to the specially selected jewel."

"I get to keep the girl. I won't leave her here, as I do when I select from your harem." I wouldn't put it past Trevolo to take my money and then expect me to leave Ana with him.

"The other guests will believe she is simply one of my harem jewels, so as long as no guest is aware you are taking her from the island, I have no objection."

I pretended to contemplate the decision and then said, "Done."

"Excellent. Now that business has concluded, let's not talk of it again and join the others."

We moved into the main area of the terrace, and I slipped my hand back in my pocket to turn off the recorder.

A tall, probably six-foot-seven, brawler of a man approached us. He had bright green eyes that were in contrast to his shock of red hair.

"Welcome to the party, I'm Silas Finn," he said with a thick Irish accent.

Silas was a known member of the Irish underground. He had a taste for blood play but was known for treasuring the women he took to bed. Once he was done, he made sure his mistresses were set for life. He wasn't one of the men to watch on this island; he stayed away from the trafficking of human cargo. It was his hard limit.

I'd also helped him establish territorial rights for the arms trade in and out of Ireland. We'd never met in person, just through representatives. I knew who he was, but I rarely let anyone see my face and match it to my cover. I shook his hand and said, "Julian Bonaparte."

He lifted a brow and then smiled. "Well, it is good to finally meet you."

"Likewise."

"At least I know there's one man here that can take care of his own business without hiding behind his protection. I can't stand soft men." He glanced in the direction of a group who looked too weak to do anything but give orders and cower behind their bodyguards.

Those were the worst of the people I wanted to take down. I could almost bet half of them were going to be buying human cargo by the end of the two weeks. The weak-minded always preyed on others, and because they were pampered princes, they believed they could use their privilege to get what they wanted.

As if on cue, they moved in our direction.

"You must be the guest Trevolo was waiting for. I'm Mica Chance," a man with a sharp angular face and too-white teeth said, offering me his hand.

Taking it, I responded, "Julian Bonaparte."

Saying my name caused the rest of the men to grow quiet. I could feel their wariness and curiosity.

At this point, I wasn't sure if the story the agency had weaved about me was a benefit or liability.

"I heard a rumor that Trevolo has picked out an item specifically for you and kept her hidden."

I gave him a deadpan look. Mica Chance seemed to fit the role of the pompous prick I'd pegged him for. I was going to have to do a little research about this man. I hadn't heard of him before, but that didn't mean much when there was a new wannabe kingpin emerging every day.

Breaking the silence from my nonresponse, Trevolo said, "Gentlemen, let's move inside. I'd like to go through the docket of auction items and answer any questions."

It took another twenty minutes to get everyone seated and settled in the lounge. Each of the twenty men invited to the island was given a folder containing pictures and statistics about the women. Some looked no older than their teens in order to cater to the guests who had fantasies about schoolgirls. I knew most of it was the clothing and the poses. Trevolo kept his harem jewels at the minimum age of eighteen. Plus, I had a reputation for despising the sale of children and happily took out anyone who engaged in it without thought. Yep, I was a criminal with a moral code.

It was probably the reason why Trevolo had kept me from the special auctions until now. Well, there was still a chance I wouldn't see the inside of the room where the sale of his special jewels would take place. My prize was in the group with his harem.

Maybe it was better that way. In all my time at the agency, I'd gone deep undercover but never to the level of sex trafficker. This wasn't something I had the stomach for, but I'd go into the bowels of hell to get Ana back.

The men around me perused the catalogue of women, *ooh*ing and *aah*ing. It was a waste of time. I wanted to see Ana, make sure she was okay.

"What has you frowning, Mr. Bonaparte?" Trevolo studied me.

I dropped the book on the table, sending a disgusted look at one of the men next to me who was ogling a naked picture of one of the girls. "I'm not interested in women posed as schoolgirls."

Trevolo smiled. "The pictures aren't to offend, just a sampling of what is available. Maybe if I show you the prize of tonight's auction, it will lighten your mood." Trevolo picked up a remote, punched a button to lower a screen from the ceiling, and turned on a camera. The image showed some kind of cell. Then in the corner, I saw her.

Anaya.

She was chained to a bed and asleep, or at least that's how it appeared. She wore a thin shirt that barely covered her body and revealed she was naked underneath. The side of her face was swollen, as if she'd been recently punched, and bruises marred her legs and arms.

I clenched my fist. How the fuck was Trevolo going to pass her off as a willing, pampered slave?

Every indication said she was there by force. Either the men looking at her were blind or didn't care.

"Who is she?" asked a man I hadn't met yet.

"A lowly assistant to a designer my wife hired. I knew from the first time I saw her that she was something special and the offer of an easier life was too much for her to resist. As you can see, she is of mixed race. I'd say Indian and Caucasian. She's beautiful, but it's her eyes that get a man. They are pure amber. Like a tiger's."

A few of the men leaned forward, examining Ana further.

The motherfucking lying bastard.

"The way you have her chained makes me believe she fights like a tiger too," another man added. "I'd like to be the one who gets the pleasure to discipline her."

"For the right price, it is a possibility." Trevolo picked up his tumbler and sipped his scotch.

Before anyone else spoke again, I asked, "How much?"

"Are you asking her starting bid? Five."

Five million. I hadn't expected that high a price. Something about the gleam in Trevolo's eyes said he had expected my reaction to Ana.

"Her pussy must be made of gold to garner a starting

bid in the millions." Mica Chance shook his head.

"She's worth every penny. Since she is a new arrival, one of you will get the first taste of her. She's not a virgin but hasn't been used. Maybe a lover here or there."

"How do you know this?" a chubby man with a receding hairline questioned.

"Our physicians examined her to check for the state of her hymen. Her life before arriving here was very sheltered. Her personality isn't the type to let just any man touch her. Although, she is quite feisty." Trevolo chuckled.

"Meaning?" I probed.

The thought of how the doctors had examined Ana added to the rage boiling under my skin. They touched her without permission, without consent.

Trevolo said with a hint of amusement, "The hellcat dislocated the first doctor's shoulder when he attempted to touch her. She agrees to come here and then becomes prudish."

"That doesn't explain the chains or the beating she has obviously received." I studied Trevolo's reaction to my words.

His brow twitched as if I'd annoyed him. "My guards intervened when she attacked the doctor. Her injuries were sustained while trying to restrain her. Afterward, we decide the chain was necessary for her safety as well as ours. A little discipline and I'm sure she'll fall into line."

Fucking liar.

I glanced at the men around the room, and all of them except Silas Finn acted as if Trevolo's answer was the truth instead of the bullshit we all knew it was.

"If she's such a problem, why not send her back? I'm sure there are plenty of women willing to trade their bodies for a life of luxury," another one of the guests I had yet to meet said. "Returning her has to be easier than disciplining her into the lifestyle."

"We gave her the option. She doesn't want to return. I believe she just needs the right type of master," Trevolo turned his attention to me. "Are you the man, Mr. Bonaparte?"

"Perhaps." I held Trevolo's gaze. "How much to buy her outright? No auction, one price."

I kept my tone cool, unemotional, detached, as if I were considering a business proposition.

There were a few grumbles from the group, but most were quiet, watching the play between Trevolo and me.

There was a smirk on his face I wanted to wipe away with my fist.

"Twenty million."

I couldn't wait until the day I put a bullet in the fucker's head.

"Done." I reached down, picked up a crystal decanter, poured myself a hefty helping of Trevolo's five-thousand-dollar scotch, and swallowed the fiery alcohol in one gulp. "Now take me to see my slave."

CHAPTER FOUR

Anaya

I woke with an excruciating throb in my head and pain shooting into my jaw.

I opened my eyes, trying my best to focus on the clock attached to the ceiling, but only blurriness filled my vision.

God, my body hurt.

The fucking guard had hit me hard enough to knock me out.

Even though I hurt like hell now, I had no regrets for punching one of the bastards and breaking his nose. He deserved it for trying to feel me up.

I knew the others had warned the idiot guard that I wasn't the usual timid, weak woman Trevolo brought for his clients, but the moron thought the fact he was twice my size would intimidate me into doing as he said.

Fucker had no idea that Jeff, my trainer and mentor at Solon, was bigger than him and ten times scarier. If I could knock Jeff on his ass, the guard was no problem. Where I'd gone wrong was not noticing the second man hiding by the door. That one had landed the punch that made me lose consciousness.

After blinking a few times, I finally got my eyes to focus. Glancing at the clock, I realized I'd slept for five hours, which meant I had another few hours before lights out.

I shifted my body, only to find my arms chained to the wall. I groaned.

I should have expected it. This was standard procedure following one of my incidents.

The first time it happened was the day I'd arrived at this prison. The house doctor had informed me that he wanted to see if I was "used" or a virgin. I'd broken his arm and dislocated his shoulder.

After that day, they'd routinely drugged me with a paralytic whenever they gave me a "health exam." They made sure I knew what was happening and wanted me to feel the invasive touch of the doctor.

The first few days after my kidnapping had been a haze. I'd been dosed with some kind of sedative that allowed me to be shuffled from one handler to the next without resistance.

I vaguely remembered hearing conversations about someone ordering my abduction. Well, the abduction of Anastasia Ashton. And it wasn't the one I'd set up with my contact...with Adrian.

My fucking cover was the reason for this whole mess. Who would want the mousy design assistant? This made no sense. I'd done everything right. The only thing that kept coming to mind was that Catarina Trevolo didn't particularly like me, but I couldn't have done anything to warrant her retaliating against me in this way.

What was wrong with me? I was trying to reason out what would cause a crazy bitch like Catarina to sell people.

The only thing I was positive about was that I'd be sold with Trevolo's human cargo shipment.

Thank God I'd been left alone in my cell since arriving at the island, with no interaction with anyone but the guards who brought me my food. Well, outside of the "medical exams."

I dropped back to the bed and closed my eyes, knowing the truth of my situation.

The longer I was here, the harder it would be to find me. And I had no idea where the hell I was. A shiver ran down my spine as a sense of resignation flooded me. I knew what my fate would be if my team didn't find me. I'd become property, sold to the highest bidder, used for God only knew what. If everything had gone according to plan, I'd have constant monitoring and backup to sweep in to get me out of anything I was in.

What would become of me if Solon didn't get to me in time?

I swallowed as bile filled my throat.

The latch on my cell clicked, and I jolted to sitting, trying to ignore the bite of the cuffs bearing down into my wrists.

A group of well-dressed men in suits walked in with Trevolo, and an avalanche of dread weighed down on me. This was it. My time was up.

"Gentlemen, this is the prize we've dubbed 'the hellcat.' She would have been the crown jewel of our auction, if Mr. Bonaparte hadn't already bought her." Trevolo spoke in English, a stark contrast to the Italian he used when he'd visited me previously.

"Bonaparte likes to hoard all the special ones. I've lost to him at least three times."

The other men began to talk around me, but all I could focus on was that someone had bought me.

Then my mind registered where I'd heard the name Bonaparte.

Julian Bonaparte was a member of a notorious arms- and drug-trafficking family. He was thought to be a genius and had unseen skills when it came to cybersecurity. He also held a reputation for cruel heartlessness in all aspects of his life. There were no second chances in his eyes. Those who crossed him rarely saw the light of the next day.

Hope slowly seeped from my soul as tears burned the back of my throat. I wrapped my arms around my bent knees and hid my face in my lap.

I can survive until Solon gets me out. I will survive until Solon gets me out.

A man at the foot of the bed reached down to touch me but stopped when I kicked out.

The group laughed.

"As I said, hellcat." The humor in Trevolo's voice made me want to do more than kick him.

"Let us at least have a look at what we have lost." The same man lifted his hand toward me again but stopped when Trevolo stepped between us.

"That is not a decision I can make. You know the rules of auctions. Mr. Bonaparte owns this jewel. He has to be willing to share his slave. After all, he did pay twenty million for her."

The group shifted, and all of a sudden, I felt a prickle of awareness that I'd only felt around one person. My heartbeat accelerated. I closed my eyes and dropped my head again, not wanting to be disappointed.

"Request denied," Adrian said, making my head snap up.

He moved through the crowd of men, toward the bed.

There was a cold edge to him I'd never seen before. One that made him seem dangerous in an almost volatile way.

He studied me, giving no indication he knew me. His gaze traveled from my feet, over the T-shirt that barely covered my body, then to my arms.

"Unchain her," he ordered. "No one is to lay a finger on her without my permission."

"You heard the man." Trevolo gestured to the guards who seemed to hesitate at the request.

The guard freed my arms and I immediately crawled to the top of the bed, away from Adrian and the men. I reacted out of instinct and tried to pull my minuscule shirt over my hips.

Adrian's gaze lingered on the dove tattoo on my hip.

"Come here, little dove," Adrian commanded. "I'd like a word with you."

But before I could shift, he grabbed me by the throat, pulling me toward him.

I whimpered as the sting of his tight hold pressed against my airway. Dear God, what was he doing?

This was not my Adrian, but Julian.

My eyes stung and my mind clouded as if I was about to pass out.

"You belong to me now, little dove. Your happiness depends on how well you please me. Behave and I will reward you, misbehave and I will punish you." His hold eased, allowing me to breathe. "From this moment on, you will do what I want, whenever I want, with whoever I want. If I say get on your knees and crawl, you will do it without question. If I tell you to lift your skirt so I can fuck you in front of a crowded room, you will do it. I won't hurt you unless you force me to. Do I make myself clear?"

His emerald green gaze bored into mine. "Y-yess," I whimpered.

I wanted to sag with relief that Adrian was here, but I couldn't. This was only the beginning.

He abruptly released me, dropping me onto the bed, and turned. I gasped for air and rolled to my side.

"Your money will be in the account within the hour. Have her cleaned up and placed in the bridal suite."

It took another few minutes before the men filed out. Each looking at me as if they had lost an unfair competition.

The door locked again, but I knew this time it wouldn't be long before someone came to get me.

The coldness of Adrian's gaze was nothing like I'd ever experienced with him before. It was as if he had totally changed personalities. I thought I was good at keeping my cover, but Adrian was beyond anything I'd seen. And from the way everyone seemed to react to him, I knew he'd established his role over a long period of time.

All that mattered was that he was on the island with me, and as sick as it sounded, he'd bought me.

I released a sigh of relief.

I would get out of here. I would get to go back to my old life.

Then a sense of guilt hit me. There were women and children hidden somewhere on this island that would never have that option.

I had to play the role of slave and find out everything I could to get them out. I couldn't be Anaya Anthony here—the only person anyone could ever see was Anastasia Ashton.

I was a purchased slave.

Adrian would use me, abuse me...I swallowed.

And share me.

From my research, it was a courtesy for a harem slave to be given to a man of the owner's choosing.

I couldn't see Adrian even considering that option. He was possessive by nature. I remembered him punching a guy at a club we'd gone to in college when he'd made a pass at me.

We would both do what we needed to get off this island, finish our assignments, and get the information needed to take down Trevolo and the men who were the buyers for his illegal slaves.

From the way the men who'd entered my cell had

spoken, I hadn't been part of the special auction but the one Trevolo conducted with his harem.

It made no sense, but there had to be a reason.

The door opened and a young woman with long blond hair entered. She wore a collar around her neck that sparkled as if covered in diamonds. As she moved closer, I realized they *were* diamonds. Then I noticed her clothes. They were designer, like the kind a wealthy woman would wear on vacation, and there wasn't a bruise on her body that I could see. She had to be from Trevolo's harem.

"Who are you?" I asked.

"I'm Ele. I'm here to prepare you for your master," she said in English with a hint of an Italian accent. She offered me her hand. "Come with me and I'll get you cleaned up."

I slid my palm over hers and wanted to weep. This was the first touch from another person in over a month I was fine with.

Keep it together, Anaya.

I followed her without any argument. We entered a hallway that led into an area with high ceilings and large windows overlooking the ocean. My breath hitched. I was definitely not in Italy anymore.

I studied the foliage, the shore, and the people working to maintain the beach. A yacht passed by in the distance and I made out the name *Caribbean Escape.*

"Are we in the Caribbean?" I asked.

"Yes." She gave me a wary look. "It's best not to ask too many questions, especially out in public."

I nodded and then noticed the cameras and guards stationed toward the end of the long walkway.

"This way." Ele gestured to a large wooden door that was probably ten feet tall.

She guided me into what I could only describe as a fairy-tale princess's bedroom. Sheer drapes flowed with the wind by the windows, a grand four-poster bed sat in the center of the room, and the walls were decorated in various pastel shades to craft the design of a garden.

"Is this my room?"

"Only for tonight. If your master is pleased with you, he will move you to his bungalow."

"And if he's not?"

She hesitated then said, "As far as the other guests know, you are one of Master Trevolo's harem jewels, sold to Mr. Bonaparte for the next two weeks. For your sake, never forget it."

"So, I'm to pretend I'm here by choice?"

"Yes. The alternative isn't something you will survive."

I studied her. "Did you make the same choice?"

She didn't look at me. "I made the choice that kept me alive."

"What are you, if not part of his harem?"

"Master Trevolo's house mistress."

What the hell did that mean?

As if reading my thoughts, she answered, "I do what Master tells me. I am his pet, his slave, and the mistress who runs the estate."

"You play the role of his wife."

Anger flashed in her brown gaze. "No, I am the woman she refuses to be for her husband. I know you met her. She is the reason Master Trevolo had any interest in you in the first place. He mentioned she wasn't very fond of you and wanted you gone."

Catarina Trevolo was a right bitch. She'd worked me like crazy and then accused me of slacking and trying to land a rich man with my flirting. When the fuck had I had time to flirt?

It made sense that Catarina was involved. The last thing I remembered was approaching the speedboat near the dock to pick up the purse she thought she'd left there. Then I'd woken up in the cell.

"Why do you look so familiar?" I studied her face. "Do I know you?"

"I'm her sister."

My stomach dropped, not believing what I was hearing.

Catarina Trevolo had sold her own sister. To her husband, at that.

"I don't understand."

"What is there to understand? It was either die or live here."

"But, what about your family?"

There was pain under her words. "They don't know what I've become."

Everything I'd researched said Catarina Trevolo came from one of the wealthiest families on the island country of Malta. Then I remembered—the middle daughter Elenora was believed dead. There were rumors of a cover-up for a kidnapping that resulted in her death.

"Please, let's not talk about it again. It's a conversation that could get both of us in trouble." Ele moved toward the bathroom. "Come. I have to prepare you for your new husband."

"Are they really going to make me marry him?"

Ele turned on the shower, dropped some kind of scented tablet on the tiled floor, and closed the glass door.

"Does it matter if there is a ceremony or not? He bought you at a bride price. That means you're a bride. It doesn't matter that the rest of the guests do not know the truth about you. Besides, your status is elevated for that mere reason. It also means more people will pay attention to you."

"I don't understand."

"Master Trevolo kept you specifically for Mr. Bonaparte."

"Why?" I asked. "What about me made me right for him?"

"Mr. Bonaparte gravitates towards women who have

your look. Master Trevolo knew without a doubt Mr. Bonaparte would pay an exorbitant price for you. Plus, the fact so many of the guests were enthralled by you adds to your value. They are referring to you as the Aphrodite of Catarina Island."

The last thing I viewed myself as was Aphrodite. Men didn't fall at my feet in love. Hell, the one I wanted had turned away from me.

"Take off your clothes. I placed eucalyptus and lavender scents in the shower. They will soothe your senses. You have thirty minutes to get ready." Ele turned in a no-nonsense way, moving to a chair by the vanity, and sat.

"You're staying?"

"Yes. I am to prepare you. After your shower, I'll fill you in on what to expect with your master."

I wanted to ask questions but thought better of it. I was desperate to take a shower and get the filth of this morning's exam off me. The few showers Trevolo allowed me had been supervised by the guards. The water had been lukewarm at best, but I'd gotten clean. The only clothing I was permitted to wear were thin white T-shirts. It was something, instead of having to be naked all the time.

I pulled the shirt from my body, throwing it on the floor, and then opened the door to the glass enclosure, stepped under the multiple sprays of the six showerheads.

I lifted my face into the water and whimpered as heat began to seep into my bones. "Oh God, this feels so good."

Bracing my hands on the wall, I let the streams cascade over my skin. If I closed my eyes, I could almost pretend I was in the center of the giant shower in the master bedroom of my apartment in Vegas.

It had been nearly four months since I'd been home, and that was in secret without my family knowing. I missed Henna, my brothers, my sisters-in-law, and I missed my nephews, two of whom I hadn't even met yet.

Why had I stayed away so long?

Adrian.

I'd avoided him like the plague and now he was the one to save me. Well, that was if we made it out of here.

"I suggest you wash before your time is up." Ele's voice snapped me out of my thoughts. "I don't want you to go into this unprepared."

I followed her instructions and washed my hair and body. As I turned off the water, Ele opened the shower door and held an oversized towel.

She wrapped it around me and led me to the seat she'd just vacated. With another towel, she began to dry my hair.

"It is your duty to gratify your master in any way he pleases. Do not argue. Do not turn from his advances. Do not let him think for one minute that you aren't grateful to be his bride."

"Can you tell me about him?"

Outside of what the CIA had put out into the world, Adrian's cover was a complete mystery to me, and it was best I had as much information as possible.

"Julian Bonaparte is the eldest son of the Bonaparte family. His father is a figurehead for the family."

"So my..." I hesitated, "...master is the actual leader of the clan?"

"Yes. He is a younger, harder version of his father." She set the towel on the floor by the chair and then moved in front of me to apply my makeup. "Do yourself a favor and don't fight him. He isn't known for second chances."

"Did you fight?"

"Yes." She nodded. "Learn from my mistakes. Resisting isn't worth weeks of unbearable pain."

"Does he still punish you?"

"Rarely. Now it's more for pleasure." Her response had a tinge of sadness.

Before I could respond, her phone beeped. She pulled it from the pocket of her pants.

"Mr. Bonaparte is on his way."

"Wait. What about the other harem women?"

"There is nothing to worry about; they know their place."

"Won't they question my sudden appearance?"

"Even if they are curious about you, they will keep their mouths shut. They chose this life and know if they displease Master Trevolo, every ounce of luxury ends."

"So they'll pretend I'm one of them?"

"Yes."

"And the others?" I probed. "I can't be the only one here against my will like this."

She opened her mouth to respond but then shut it.

After a few seconds, she said, "The only person you need to worry about is you. As I said earlier, never let anyone know you are here other than by your choice."

She offered me her hands to help me up. She lifted a long-sleeved sheer gown from a nearby hanger and helped me slip it on. After lighting a series of candles around the room, she went to the balcony doors, opening them to let in the sound of the ocean.

If this were a different situation, I'd almost think the setting was romantic, with the breeze moving the lightweight curtains and the glow of the many tea lights around the room.

"Pleasing him is your priority. He will treat you like a treasure as long as you do as he says. I will come to you in the morning."

Ele moved to the door, leaving me inside the opulent room to wait for Adrian.

CHAPTER FIVE

Adrian

I entered the bridal suite to find Ana sitting in the center of a giant four-poster bed.

God, she was the most beautiful thing I'd ever seen. The glow of the candlelight around her made her look otherworldly.

Her head was bowed, and her long dark blond hair was damp and cascading down her back. She wore an almost see-through gown of ivory, giving her a virginal aura.

She lifted her face, hitting me with the impact of those amber eyes of hers. They were no longer glazed with pain or drugs. The bruising on the side of her face was more evident than before, but it didn't detract from her beauty. It made her look more fragile, breakable.

I wanted to wrap her in my arms and take her away, pretend these five years had never happened. Ana brought out a protective streak in me that I'd never experienced with any other woman. I'd had female partners before and had no problems watching their back and trusting them to watch mine. I'd always believed women in the agency were as good and sometimes better than the men. They had less egos and because of the bureaucracy of the system, more to prove.

But with Anaya Anthony, my inner caveman wanted to come out, take her away, hide her, protect her. It wouldn't matter that she was strong or deserved the chance to protect herself.

She was mine. Always had been and always would be. Being apart hadn't changed it.

She watched me as I closed the door, locking it behind me, and walked toward her. She remained quiet, waiting to see what I'd do.

I unbuttoned and shrugged off my shirt, throwing it on a nearby chair.

Her breath hitched. I glanced down and I knew she was studying the tattoos covering most of the left side of my body, from my shoulder, down my ribs, to my waist.

If she examined the patterns close enough, she'd see the scars hidden underneath, ones I'd received less than a month after breaking things off with her, ones that made me positive at the time that I'd done the right thing.

I stopped at the foot of the bed. "You're mine now."

She continued to gaze at me, not saying a word.

"Come here."

She hesitated then crawled to where I stood, and then sat back on her knees, hands resting on her thighs, and head bowed.

My cock jumped.

Fuck. This was my fantasy come to life. If only it was in another place, another time.

"Look at me." When she followed my command, I said, "Everything you knew is gone. I won't hurt you, Anastasia, unless you force me to. Do you understand?"

"Yes," she whispered, her voice raspy.

I sat down, patting my lap. She didn't move. I repeated the motion and waited. After a few seconds, Ana shifted to straddle me with her thighs, pooling her gown around us and setting her hands on my bare shoulders. I knew she felt my erection against her naked pussy, but I couldn't help it. I was always rock hard whenever she was near me.

My hands gripped her waist and we stared at each other. Then her eyes looked at various points in the room.

I nodded.

She was as aware of the cameras as I was. Trevolo liked to record the first encounters with his buyers and the slaves purchased. It was his version of live-action porn. At a price of twenty million, I knew it was too much to expect for Trevolo to garner me some privacy.

I hated the shithead, but getting Ana out of here was the priority, and to do that, I had to play the game. *We* had to play the game. And if we survived, I was going to take great pleasure in killing the bastard.

Leaning toward her ear, I bit her lobe and then whispered so only she could hear, "I've disabled the audio, but we have to still be careful."

Her fingers tightened on my shoulders as she released a relieved breath.

"This isn't how I wanted it between us, but we don't have a choice," I murmured. "I won't be like before. I'll expect things of you. Make you do things... I can't be gentle."

She paused my words with her quiet, almost inaudible response. "Was it ever gentle between us?"

She was right. Our sexual encounters had always had a mix of domination and submission. It had come naturally to us. It was as if we read each other's needs without vocalizing what they were. We'd experimented and done almost everything imaginable between a couple.

"They gave me your report. How long has it been, Ana?"

She dropped her face, looking away. She knew what I was asking.

I tilted her chin back up with a finger. "I asked you a question."

"Five years." Her lips trembled and I knew what she'd left out: *"With you."*

A fist gripped my heart and squeezed.

She hadn't been with anyone since a week after that fateful night in a Las Vegas chapel.

I had so many questions, most of all *why*, but they'd have to wait until we moved to my bungalow on the shore. The one place on the island without surveillance. That would be at least a week from now.

As if feeling the intensity of what she'd admitted, her eyes filled with tears.

I cupped her jaw, rubbing my thumb over her lower lip. Her breathing grew unsteady and her nails dug into my skin.

I leaned down to take her mouth but stopped the second the sound of a camera moving reached my ears.

Motherfucker was watching us live. The anger I had boiling inside me felt as if it would erupt. I knew anything Ana and I did in this house would be viewable, but I hadn't realized how much of a visceral reaction I'd have knowing anyone would see Ana the way I saw her.

I glared up at the camera, ready to walk out of the room and give the bastard a piece of my mind. I shifted my hands to lift Ana off me; however, before I could move, Ana spoke, drawing my attention away from the camera.

"Ele said I had to please you or..." She trailed off, giving me a hint of fear. "Let me please you."

The plea in her gaze got me to focus. *I am here for a reason, to get Ana out of here and finish the mission.*

I was Julian, not Adrian, and she was Anastasia, not Anaya.

God, she deserved so much better than this.

I gripped her nape and said, "You want to please me?"

"Yes." Her voice quivered, in a way that wasn't just for show.

It didn't matter that we were in a fucked-up situation or that it was a job, nothing between us was ever just business. She knew it as much as I did.

I drew her forward and covered her mouth with mine.

My kiss was bruising, filled with anger, passion, and need. Need for the woman I'd lost so long ago, need for the life we couldn't have because of our ages and our dreams, and most of all, need for the love of the only being who ever held my heart.

"You fucking taste incredible." I deepened the embrace, pushing my tongue past her lips. She gave a cry of protest before giving in.

Only to bite my lip, surprising the fuck out of me.

"What the fuck was that for?" I grabbed her jaw, squeezing it tight, probably tighter than I needed to.

Her fingers gripped my wrist and her eyes dilated as a slight whimper escaped her lips and her breath came out in short pants.

God, how could I forget? She loved it when I was rough, giving her that slight bite of pain.

"Behave." I gritted my teeth, feeling the slick heat of her pussy dampening my fabric-covered, straining cock.

Her pleasure, her need, her arousal were supposed to be private, for me only. Not for a fucking camera or the pervert who was watching us.

With anyone else I wouldn't have thought twice. They would have been a job, but she was anything but.

"Do you understand?" I loosened my hold on her jaw long enough to gain her agreement, then I took her lips again. I plundered her mouth, gorging, losing myself in the incredible taste of her lips.

Breaking our kiss, I stared at her, gasping for air.

"I want you naked." Releasing her face, I reached down, grabbed the hem of her gown, and tossed it over her head and onto the floor.

Her skin was a light golden hue marred by too many bruises to count. Then I noticed two small, jagged, uneven scars, one on her shoulder and another near her lower ribs. Both had the distinct markings of emergency surgery. They were old, healed, and had a story.

Were they bullet wounds or something else?

"You will be telling me all about those." I couldn't hide the demand of my tone.

Her fingers trailed over the scars under my tattoos. She didn't have to say it for me to hear, *"Ditto."*

Her light touch over the sensitive skin had goosebumps running down my spine.

I slid my palms over her breasts, squeezing, kneading the full round mounds. Ana had always had the most perfect breasts.

I kissed down her neck, supporting her back as I tilted her until I could suck the puckered and straining bud of her nipple into my mouth. I licked, lapped, teased.

God, I missed touching her.

"Ohh," she cried out as I bit her sensitive nub before blowing on it and moving to the other breast.

She held on to my forearms, arching into the caress of my lips and tongue. My cock was on the verge of exploding. Her little shifts matched with her moans were driving me insane.

She was always a fucking goddess when she was lost in need.

I'd have to bury my cock in her soon. It had been so long. I'd go slow another time, when I could worship her the way she deserved, when we were alone in my bungalow and no cameras were present.

I tugged her toward me, standing up and sliding her down my body until her feet touched the floor.

We were both breathing heavily.

"Undress me."

She hesitated, holding her fists closed by her sides.

"I gave you an order."

She remained still and just when I thought I'd have to do something to discipline her, she reached for the belt at my waist, tugging the leather open, unbuttoning and pushing down my slacks, and freeing my cock. I stepped out of my pants, shoving them to the side with a foot.

She stared down at the engorged head of my erection, her breath grew heavy, and any pretense of not wanting me seemed to vanish from her demeanor. She'd always had a fascination with my cock, enjoying sucking me off as much as I had.

She licked her lips. Precum wept from the tip, and it would only get worse if she kept looking at me with hunger. I'd spent so many nights dreaming about feeling the heat of her mouth on me, of her working me, hitting the back of her throat with my thrusts, of her swallowing everything I gave her.

"Kneel down and lick it."

Her eyes shifted to the camera for a brief moment and then she inhaled deep, dropping to the floor.

Her fingers gingerly touched my hips as she moved forward and ran her tongue up the dripping slit on the tip of my cock.

Fuck. That felt good.

Before I could tell her to do anything else, she engulfed my length into her heated, wet mouth. I grabbed her head in a tight hold and forced her forward to take all of me.

She gagged, not expecting the move. I pulled out and

brought her forward again, chuckling as she choked again, playing into my bastard role.

I hated treating her like this, but I had no choice.

"Too much for you, little dove? Better get used to it. I plan to fuck your mouth often and I expect you to take all of me."

This time as I brought her forward, she swallowed, opening the back of her throat to accommodate me, breathing through her nose.

"Ahh. Good girl. You're learning." I let her suck me a few more times before jerking her back by her hair. "As much as I want to shoot down your throat, tonight I want to come in that pussy. Soon it's going to curve to the shape of my dick."

She gazed up at me through tear-soaked lashes, lips swollen, mouth dripping with saliva, and skin flushed.

"Come here. I want to feel your tight cunt wrapped around my cock."

Releasing her hair, I sat on the bed. She tried to pull away, but I tugged her toward me, forcing her thighs apart to straddle my hips. Arousal smeared the skin of her inner thighs and the little pearl of her clit poked out from between her pussy lips.

God. Pretending that she didn't want me got her off. I was going to die before this night was out.

My cock strained upward, and I resisted the urge to slam up into her. I grabbed the base, sliding my palm up and down and then twirling the head of my dick through her soaked slit, coating it with her arousal.

I positioned myself at the entrance to her core, eagerly waiting for the ecstasy of her body to surround me.

"Take me inside you, Ana."

She held her dripping pussy rigid over my straining cock, desire mixed with worry clouding her fiery depths.

"What is it?" I couldn't help the harshness of my response. I was on the edge.

"I missed my Depo shot. I could get..." She trailed off.

Fisting her hair, I jerked her face toward me as my other hand released my cock and gripped her hip. "There are no other options. You're my bride."

Desire cooled from her amber gaze. "You can't change your mind once it happens."

She may have whispered those words, but she couldn't hide the pain from the past lacing them. I wished I could take it away, but I'd had no choice at the time. Maybe if we survived this, then she'd understand the reason our lives had to go the way they did.

"You're mine. You were born mine. Whatever happens, it was meant to be." With those last words, I thrust up and simultaneously pulled her onto me.

She cried out at the invasion as I groaned in bliss.

God, she felt incredible. She was so tight. Her small, slick cunt wrapped around me like a fist.

Five fucking years, I'd waited for her.

I resisted the urge to flip her on her back and rut into her like a madman. We'd always used protection in the past, not wanting to risk anything while we were still in college. Going bare was like a piece of heaven on earth.

After a few seconds, her pussy relaxed its hold on my cock, getting used to my girth.

She released a slight whimper, reminding me of our first time together.

The vision of that long-ago night flashed in my head. Before our elopement, before the job with the CIA, or Ana's internship. It was the summer after my senior year and her sophomore year at the University of Nevada-Las Vegas. We'd been seeing each other in secret for nearly a year, knowing our families would flip if they ever found out.

Outside of the fact we were so young and in such a serious relationship, Ana's brothers had just learned Ana was their half sister, and Penny and I were dealing with the craziness following my mother's arrest for too many crimes to even think about. Ana and I had found comfort in each other's arms, something I treasured to this day.

Her pussy relaxed, and she shifted from side to side, making me grit my teeth.

"Oh." She rose up and lowered with small shallow movements, her pussy sucking me in further and further.

She was going to kill me. I had to maintain control.

"Hold your arms at the base of your back and ride me."

Her lips parted as if to argue, but then she conceded. I gripped her neck as she lifted up and then slid down my cock. Her movements were slow and controlled. That was until my thumb grazed her clit.

She bucked at the first touch and cried out, "It's too much. I can't."

"I will tell you when it is too much."

Her face was a play of anguish and pleasure as she lifted again. This wasn't something she hadn't experienced with me before. Though it was night-and-day gentler than what my reputation was with Trevolo. Soon I'd have to use her, fuck her, and share her, all in the hopes of getting off this island with her.

She wasn't ready for the world she belonged to now.

"Do I make myself clear?"

She nodded. "Yes."

"Good. Now I want to fuck."

She rode me, hypnotizing me with the sway of her breasts and the slight way her lips parted as I filled her with each downward glide.

Her pussy quickened and my dick was flooded with her desire. I continued to torment her aching clit with light grazes, circles, and flicks.

"Oh God. Oh God. Oh God." She threw her head back, biting her bottom lip and squeezing her eyes tight.

I held her down, rubbing the base of my cock against her sensitive tissues, and then smacked her ass.

The heat from the contact and Ana's whine had my dick growing harder.

"You said you wouldn't hurt me," she gritted out.

"There is a difference and you know it. The fact your cunt just spasmed tells me you wouldn't object to a spanking."

I knew for a fact she loved a good spanking. There had been times she'd begged for it.

Anger flared in her golden gaze. "No spankings. I'm not a child."

"You don't get to tell me no. Your life, your pleasure, your pain are mine. I won't repeat myself anymore."

I cupped her throat in the same way I'd done in her cell, drawing her forward.

Understanding registered as she released a ragged breath. We were running a thin knife's edge between the desire we shared and acting for the cameras.

I lifted her, letting all but the head of my cock slip from her heat, and then dropped her down. I gripped her forearms, pressing her wrists against her beautiful round ass.

"Now ride me. Show me that I own you. And don't even think about coming unless I give you permission."

For the next few minutes, she undulated her hips as she moved up and down. Her mesmerizing eyes held mine hostage. Her breathing was unsteady, and sweat beaded her face, neck, and chest.

I refused to let her come until she begged. It had to happen this way, for her sake and mine. Even if we didn't have eyes on us, I'd have made her beg. She'd always wanted that release of control and with me she'd gotten it.

I hissed as her pussy contracted around me, pushing my ability to resist the demands of her body.

She bit her lip a second before a sob of need escaped. "Please. Please. Please. I need to come."

I couldn't hide my satisfied grin.

I dropped my hold on her arms, positioning her hands around my neck, then spread her thighs wide, thrusting up and grinding against her clit.

She detonated, clamping down on me and losing her balance. Her sweat-soaked body pressed against mine and her hard-as-pebbles nipples rubbed my chest with each thrust.

I pumped up into her, keeping the tempo to prolong her orgasm. "Who am I?"

"I..." She caught herself and then said, "My master."

"Who owns you?"

"You do." She bit down on my shoulder, and my control snapped.

I flipped her onto her back, pulled her legs apart, and thrust deep. I pounded her, hard and fast. She moaned and begged, clawing at my back for a second release.

I grabbed her wrists, pinning them above her head.

"Please," she whimpered. "Please."

"Say, 'Please, Master, let me come.'" I would rather have her say my name, but this scene was pushing it.

"P-p-please, Master, let me come."

I slid my fingers between us and rolled her swollen clit. I continued fucking her as I worked her aching bundle of nerves. When I knew she wouldn't be able to control her release any longer, I gave her the roll of my hips that I knew would send her over.

"Come now."

She gasped and then screamed, clenching around me in rhythmic spasms. She thrashed and bucked, lost in her orgasm. A few seconds later I followed, coming harder than any other time in the last five years.

CHAPTER SIX

Anaya

"Time to wake up," I heard Ele say as she drew the curtains open.

I winced as sunlight slashed over my face and ducked my head under the covers. My body ached from the marathon sex I'd had with Adrian. How could I have forgotten the man was a machine and could go almost all night, and the more he came, the longer he went the next round. I'd barely fallen asleep the last time before he lifted my leg and thrust into me from behind, fucking me until I came at least two times.

I shifted to the side and moaned. One thing was for sure, Adrian's stamina was insane, and it hadn't waned with age.

He'd been rough and demanding, at times pushing me so far that I begged to sleep. This wasn't Adrian, the lover who would never push me past my limits, but Julian, a man who didn't stop until he was satisfied.

He'd reminded me of it when he'd slipped out of the bed a little before dawn and whispered against my ear, "Ana, I'm not Adrian, I'm Julian. For your life and mine, don't ever forget it. You are my reluctant slave."

You are my reluctant slave.

"You must get up. I have orders to bring you to the dining room for breakfast."

I pushed out from under the comforter to look at Ele, who was busily moving about the room. She opened a cabinet, pulling out ballet flats that I was positive were my size, and then went inside the bathroom and came out with a floor-length dress in pale green, setting it on the bed. It didn't go unnoticed to me that I wasn't given any underwear.

"The fact you are able to move at all is a good thing. Don't delay and cause yourself grief."

Slipping out of the bed, I went to brush my teeth, but paused when I noticed the aura of agitation surrounding Ele.

"Is something wrong?"

Ele stopped arranging my clothes on the bed. "Everything is fine."

That was when I noticed the bruise forming on the side of Ele's cheek.

"Will you help me turn on the shower?" I asked, trying to get her in the bathroom. "I'd love more of the scents you added yesterday."

Ele glanced in the direction of one of the cameras and nodded.

I used the bathroom and brushed my teeth as Ele prepared the shower.

Before she closed the glass door, I touched her cheek and she flinched.

"Do they listen to our conversations?"

"The bedroom is recorded, voice and video." She opened a cabinet to pull out a round ball that smelled like lavender.

She opened the glass door, dropped the ball near the drain, and turned on the shower before turning to me.

"The only place to speak in the house is the bathrooms —well, most of them."

I had to assume this one was safe since she was speaking so freely.

Ele continued, "However, Mr. Bonaparte disabled audio for the entire suite the second he entered the room. Master discovered it when he decided to observe your wedding night."

I was so glad Adrian had told me he'd cut the audio. It was hard enough letting others see my most intimate of moments without the added worry of them hearing everything.

"Did this cause problems?"

"No. Mr. Bonaparte is too valuable to upset. Plus, it is well known that Mr. Bonaparte has the technical skills to shut down all technology on the island with a few computer commands."

"He's a hacker? I thought you said he was head of his family's business."

"Mr. Bonaparte has many skills. They say he is some type of genius and that's the reason he took over his family's operations at such a young age."

Adrian's genius was on a level like no one else. He'd started hacking when he was a teen as a way to avoid spending time with his crazy, controlling mother. I used to joke that it was his sister Penny's fault for enrolling him in programming classes. Then again, Penny was a prodigy in her own right, so it had to run in the family.

Ele moved to a closet and pulled out towels. "I saw the video. He was patient with you and gentle at times."

"Is that unexpected?"

"Mr. Bonaparte doesn't like to repeat himself. His temper is well known."

"What does that mean? He beats women?"

"No. Discipline is only something he uses on occasion and the women he takes prefer his methods to others. Mr. Bonaparte is skilled."

Jealousy shot through the back of my mind.

"He wasn't gentle with me." My body ached from the level of *not gentle* he was.

"Compared to other men on the island he was. Count yourself lucky. But don't expect it to continue."

"Why?"

"Master Trevolo believes Mr. Bonaparte was seducing you into your new life." She studied me and then said, "Never forget that they will watch everything you do the second you step out of this suite. You made the most dangerous man on the island gentle for you."

"Dangerous? How?"

"I can't go into details, just know the rumors about Mr. Bonaparte aren't false. No one crosses him without consequences."

"I'm sure he has many enemies."

"This world is full of rivalries, but everyone has a role. Enemies will conduct business because it is mutually beneficial."

"What about here?"

"Same rules. Mr. Bonaparte willingly shares his women with his biggest rivals in the outside world. One of them being Mr. Sebastian Weber."

I gripped the back of a nearby chair. "What?"

"Mr. Bonaparte has preferences—women who are submissive, who bend to domination. He enjoys...I think the English word is..." she paused, "...kink."

The thought of all he'd done with other women made me feel sick. I knew all about his preferences. Hell, we'd explored them together.

How many women had Adrian fucked here?

Calm the fuck down, Ana. He's an agent, deep undercover. You know the rules. You have to be the devil to take down the empire of the other devils.

If only logic trumped the anger burning inside my heart.

"Does he attend auctions often?"

"Occasionally. He usually gets the prized girls. Though he's never taken a bride before yesterday."

"What does 'bride' mean?"

"It means you were bought without an actual auction taking place or the chance for anyone to counteroffer."

"Does that mean he is going to take me with him or do I have to stay here?"

This thought nagged at the back of my mind. I wasn't a true harem slave but, then again, nothing with this situation had gone according to plan.

"He will take you with him, but no one is to know about it and it will have to wait until the other guests have left the island."

"Where will he take me?"

"I cannot be sure, but I can assume it will be to his estate in Cyprus. It is rumored he has a harem of his own there."

The CIA had created a seriously notorious cover for Adrian. Not only was he a crazy-as-fuck arms dealer with a temper, but a playboy on top of it.

How much of his actions on the island had played into his image?

I must have been frowning because Ele moved toward me, setting her hand on my shoulder. "You are his bride. That gives you status. He paid too much for you to let anyone treat you badly."

I knew she was trying to console me, but she had no idea that my mind was whirling from the harem thing.

"And one more thing. Don't ever forget what I told you last night. No one is to know the truth of how you arrived."

I nodded.

"Take your shower or we'll both get in trouble. I'm not allowed to be alone with you longer than necessary. Yesterday was an exception to get you comfortable. You have ten minutes to shower and meet me outside your door."

With those words, she left me.

I couldn't move. All I could envision was Adrian with countless women, of him doing things with them that he'd done with me, of him giving them the kind of pleasure he'd brought me. For five years, I hadn't been with anyone else or wanted anyone else. Yes, it was my fault. I'd been so devastated by our breakup that I'd thrown myself into my work. Plus, the thought of a random hookup just to relieve sexual frustration wasn't something that appealed to me.

God, I had no right to judge what he'd done for work. Hell, I'd been planning to do the same damn thing.

I couldn't deny the truth of my feelings. I'd never been one to lie to myself. It hurt so much because I still loved him. I'd probably love him even after we went our separate ways once we left this island. He'd go back to his man-whoring for the CIA and I'd go back to Vegas.

The last month in almost-isolation had taught me that I needed to be around people. *My* people. My family. I'd run away because of Adrian. It hadn't been fair to Henna or my brothers.

I stripped out of my clothes and quickly showered and dressed. I didn't bother with drying my hair, since I'd lost too much time in my thoughts; instead, I chose to fasten it into a bun at my nape.

Opening the door to the suite, I was met by two men, who I could only assume were guards, and Ele.

"Your master is waiting for you."

CHAPTER SEVEN

Adrian

I leaned against the balcony outside the formal dining room of the estate, staring at the waves and the birds diving for their meals. The air was balmy, thick with heat and humidity. Nothing like the dry desert air of Vegas. I would give anything to be home again, spending time with Penny and my hyper nephews. They had no idea the type of work I'd done over the last five years and hopefully they'd never find out. Hell, even the Lykaios brothers, including Hagen, my brother-in-law and Penny's husband, had no clue the depth of what I did for the CIA.

I'd become a mobster worse than anything Hagen's former boss could imagine being. Yes, ninety percent of what I was rumored to have done was bullshit and I'd fabricated my strategically planted accounts around the world. But the other ten percent was all true. I'd orchestrated arms and drug deals, collecting favors from some of the most notorious and dangerous fuckers in the world. And I'd bought women, fucked them, and negotiated deals with other buyers, just to get closer to the objective of the assignment.

Find the traffickers and take them down.

This whole thing went deeper than the typical mobster or drug lord. It involved the upper crust of the world.

It was going to get back to Ana that I was a regular at these "pleasure weeks." I really hoped she'd understand. After all, she'd been going to do the same thing if everything had gone according to plan.

I clenched my teeth. Maybe that wasn't the best example. Just the image of one of my colleagues in my place made me want to stab someone.

We'd been each other's firsts, and for some God-knew-what reason, I'd been her only.

I wasn't sure how I was going to be able to treat her like any other woman I'd bought when she was so important to me. Though the idea of binding her, flogging her, and fucking her was a fantasy I'd indulged in over and over throughout the years.

I knew she'd be my wife from the moment she walked off the plane from Arizona to start her freshman year at UNLV. It had been almost electric the way I felt when our eyes connected. We'd interacted over the years because of her relationship to Penny, with a bit of harmless flirting, but that fateful day, I knew Anaya Serina Anthony was mine. It had taken another six months before I convinced her to go out with me. She'd always been so cautious, never letting anyone close besides her sister, Henna, Penny, and Collin Lykaios.

I understood her resistance. She was, after all, the daughter of a notorious embezzler, Victor Anthony. But later I'd learned she was the product of an affair between Victor and Rhea Lykaios, wife to Collin and mother of the Lykaios brothers. It took another few years for her brothers to learn the truth.

To this day, all the world knew was that she was Victor and his wife Lena's daughter.

"So is it true what I heard? Is Julian Bonaparte whipped by Aphrodite's pussy?" Mica Chance came over with a cup of coffee in his hand.

I kept my gaze on the landscape and said, "Her name is Anastasia Ashton, and her pussy is not your business."

He laughed. "Possessiveness doesn't suit you. Wouldn't want anyone to think a Bonaparte was weakened by his affection for a woman."

Before the asshole could make another remark, I twisted, and in two moves, knocked Mica to the ground and pressed the heel of my shoe against his airway. "Do you consider this weakness? Just because I don't have a knife or gun in my hands doesn't mean I can't kill you in a matter of seconds."

I increased the pressure, making Mica choke on his spit.

"What I do and don't do with my possessions is not your concern. All you need to know is that if any hint of a rumor reaches my ears conveying the sentiment you expressed, I will take care of every single man on this island. Gossip and rumors are a disease and the only way to get rid of it is to carve it out, piece by piece." I glared down at him and then glanced at the crowd that had gathered. "Do I make myself clear?"

"Y-y-yes." Mica clutched at my shoe, responding, but the warning was for every man watching.

Releasing Mica, I walked over his wheezing body.

Trevolo stepped in front of me. "I apologize for Mr. Chance's behavior. It won't happen again."

"See that it doesn't." I moved around him, deciding it was time to find my bride.

As I passed through the doorway, I heard Trevolo say, "You dumb fuck. Bonaparte will end you without thinking twice. All of you heard his warning. Don't fuck with him. And don't for one minute think you are strong enough to take him on. He will come for you when you least expect it."

Satisfied with Trevolo's response, I moved into the atrium. My temper was in full force and wouldn't ease until I saw Ana. I stalked through toward the hallway leading to the bridal suite. Just as I turned the corner, I was intercepted by the house mistress, Ele.

She'd lost weight since the last time I'd been on the island. I'd put her on the list for Sebastian to extract a year ago, but getting her out would be beyond complicated. She was Trevolo's personal pet. No one touched her unless he invited them to join him. The fact she was his barely twenty-one-year-old sister-in-law made me want to shoot him in the head, along with Trevolo's bitch wife.

"Mr. Bonaparte, your bride is in the library waiting for you. When you weren't in the dining room, I thought it better to keep her separated from the other guests, for her safety and theirs."

Ele was smart, smarter than anyone knew. She'd done what she had to in order to survive and kept a log of every man who visited the island on a tablet she'd hidden in the bathroom of her private quarters. I'd only discovered it while scanning the island for unauthorized electronics. When I'd confronted her about it, I'd come to her as Julian Bonaparte. We'd agreed she would keep the tally for me in exchange for protection for her younger sister who was still in Malta.

"Thank you, Elenora."

Ele knew most of the men here hated my guts and would go out of their way to lure my slave away.

It hadn't worked before and would definitely not work with Ana.

Besides, the last thing I wanted to deal with was punishing Ana for breaking the nose of someone who tried to take liberties with her.

"There is a new list ready," she murmured as she turned to walk in the opposite direction of where I had to go.

Well, that just complicated things.

A new list meant new buyers and more planned auctions.

Fuck. I ran a hand through my hair. I'd have to report this.

I made my way to the library to find Ana perusing the books. Her deceptively delicate finger stroked the spines of various hardbacks. I could still feel the way she'd stroked her hands over my cock, pumping it until she had me all but mad with need.

Her wet blond hair was bound into a bun, making it look darker and closer to her natural color. As she moved about, I noticed how transparent her gown was. I could see the silhouette of her perfect breasts and the shadow of her dark nipples.

My cock immediately woke as did annoyance, knowing others would see what was mine.

As if sensing me watching her, she looked toward the doors.

Fire flashed in her golden amber gaze.

"Something wrong, Bride?"

She ignored me, turning her attention back to the books. She clenched her fists and closed her eyes, taking steadying breaths.

What the hell had I done? When I'd left her earlier in the morning she was recovering from an orgasm.

I moved in her direction, turning on the device in my pocket that would disable all feeds in this room, audio and visual. I left the door open just in case anyone passed by. I expected someone to check on us, and it would be too suspicious if I closed it.

Stopping when I was next to her, I asked, "Ana, want to tell me why you're upset?"

She pulled out a book, opening it. I plucked it from her grasp and set it on the table near us.

She scowled up at me.

"You're angry. Want to fill me in on what changed from the time I slipped out of our bed to now?"

Instead of responding, she lifted her arm and punched me in the face.

CHAPTER EIGHT

Anaya

"What the fuck was that for?" Surprise and anger colored Adrian's face.

He shifted backward and before I could land my second punch, he had his giant hand over mine, twisting my wrist in a painful grip and turning me so my back was to his front. "You're not the only one trained to fight, little dove."

His cock was hard, pressed to my ass. I gasped as a tingle went through my core and ignited anger at wanting him so much. It had always been like this. One touch from him and I was wet. If it wasn't for his huge cock, I'd forgo foreplay just to have him push inside me in one hard swoop.

God, what the hell am I thinking? I've lost my mind.

"You're sick to get off on manhandling me."

"I could say the same for you. I bet if I slid my fingers between your legs, they'd come out soaked with your need. As they were every time I fucked you last night."

I tried to steady my breath in hopes of getting my temper and hormones under control.

"Cat got your tongue?"

Before he could make another remark, I let my body go limp, almost slipping from his hold. But he was able to grab my hair a second before I hit the ground and could roll away.

I screamed as the pain shot through my scalp, and clawed at his arm.

"Dammit, Ana. I don't want to hurt you," Adrian muttered so only I could hear. "What the hell has gotten into you?"

I tried to kick out, but he shifted so fast, I caught nothing but air.

"Submit."

"No." I threw out my leg again; this time I grazed his shin. But the bastard didn't flinch or budge.

His grip intensified, bringing tears to my eyes. "If you don't yield, I will take you in front of anyone who passes by. I was patient with you last night, but that does not translate into today."

I heard his warning about the door and that he was Julian right now.

That was the point. I needed him to be Julian. Yes, I was pissed about the women, and this was the best way to channel my temper.

"Fuck you."

"That's the idea."

Adrian shifted his grip to the back of my neck, unaffected by my nails scraping his skin. He forced me forward until I was bent over a large table overlooking the ocean and pushed my cheek against the cool, polished wood.

"Now tell me what the fuck has gotten into you."

"I know about your harem." My voice was angry, filled with rage.

"Ahh, someone's been talking to you. Jealous, my little dove?"

"Of the fact you're a man-whore? No," I bit out. "I'm more worried about whether you're clean or not."

Shit, I shouldn't have said that. That was Anaya talking, not Anastasia.

He leaned over me as he jerked my dress up, exposing my naked ass, and then kicked my legs apart. "I've already had your cunt clamped around my cock completely bare. Multiple times, in fact. You'll just have to trust me."

The sound of a zipper lowering had my heart racing and my pussy quivering.

Damn traitorous body.

Adrian's thick, blunt head slid between the lips of my pussy.

Oh God, he was really going to fuck me here, in the library, where anyone could walk in?

Wasn't this the reason you punched him? To make it believable, to be the reluctant slave.

He rimmed my sex and pulled out. "You misbehaved. That means you'll be punished."

I closed my eyes, trying to resist the urge to push back and impale myself on his thick, hard length.

"I can take anything you give me."

"Is that so?" Adrian slid his cock to my clit, circling the sensitive bundle of nerves. Round and round. "Grip the edge of the table."

Without thinking, I followed his directions.

Smack.

"Ow." I whimpered, releasing my hold on the table. "That hurts."

I refused to focus on the spasms shooting through my core.

"It was meant to hurt."

Smack. Smack. Smack.

I jerked with each strike, clawing at the hand holding my neck against the table and resisting the need to moan as the sting on my ass grew to a heated ache.

"I hate you."

"Hate me all you want. You will submit."

"No, I won't," I gritted out through clenched teeth.

"Then you'll suffer the consequences."

Smack, smack, smack.

Fucking hell. That hurt. My bottom was on fire and my damn body was beyond aroused.

You're not supposed to show that you like this, Anaya.

"Next time you even think to punch me, I'll spank you, completely naked in front of everyone in the lounge, and then make you suck me off."

"No."

"You don't get to tell me no. I own you, Ana. Your pleasure and your pain are mine. I will make it clear to you and everyone else that you belong only to me."

"I belong to no man."

I expected his palm to land again but instead he slammed into me. His giant, rigid cock pushed into my aching, swollen tissue and grazed my tender, bruised ass.

"Oh God." The feel of him mixed with the adrenaline from our battle was a heady mix of pleasure and pain.

He pulled out and plunged back in while holding me in place on the table with my neck.

He rode me hard, not relenting in his pace.

My body responded to each slide of his cock. He rubbed purposefully against the charged bundle of nerves deep in my core. He knew exactly how to get me to come. He worked in and out of me, and just as I was about to go over, he stopped moving, coming in hard jerks inside me.

"Oh fuck, fuck, fuck." He worked out the last of his ejaculation and then dropped his weight against my sore ass.

I gasped, ready to cry. My muscles continued to quiver around his softening cock desperate for an orgasm that wasn't going to come.

"You bastard."

"That may be, but you're the one who won't get to come again until you've earned it."

He released my neck, pulling free of my body and tugging my dress down.

His cum dripped down my inner thighs, and I turned my head to glower at him, but stopped.

In the doorway stood Trevolo and a few of the men who'd come into my cell. Lust glazed their eyes as my cheeks heated. They'd watched Adrian fuck me.

I shifted my attention to Adrian.

"Fix yourself. It's time to start our day."

He tugged me up, positioning me behind him as he moved toward the door.

"You've had your show. Now get lost. I need to have a word with my bride."

Trevolo smirked. "I see what you're doing. You're smart to break her in slowly. Only an idiot damages a twenty-million-dollar toy the first time he plays with it."

I clenched my jaw. I wanted to stalk toward that cocky asshole and kick his teeth in.

"I look forward to seeing the lessons you will teach the little hellcat."

Trevolo and the rest of the men with him moved down the hall, leaving Adrian and me alone.

Adrian closed the door, locking it. He dropped his forehead against the wood.

He was quiet but I felt a volatile energy radiating from him.

"Master?" I stayed in my spot by the table where he'd fucked me.

"Quiet. Don't say another word."

I wanted to argue but did as he said.

After what felt like hours, he faced me. "I am going to do things to you that will make you hate me. What just happened is mild. You're strong, Ana, but this isn't anything you've ever encountered."

Why was he talking so freely? Wasn't he worried about the cameras?

He had to have seen my shock and said, "I rarely let anyone record anything about me. Everyone accepts it as part of my personality—well, Julian's. Trevolo knows I have ways to hack his security and won't think twice about doing it."

"But last night?"

"I allowed it as a way of showing Trevolo respect for

garnering me a bride. The last thing I want is for another man to see any part of you, to let anyone touch you. But we don't have a choice if I'm going to get you out of here. I can't lose you again." Adrian frowned, shaking his head. "It nearly killed me to walk away five years ago and double when I found you missing in Italy. I will fucking burn this place down before I let anyone take you from me again."

His words hit me like a punch to the heart. He still loved me, or close to it. I wanted to demand why he'd ended things the way he had, but this wasn't the time or place.

He came in my direction and stopped a mere foot from me. I lifted my hand to touch the light bruise forming on his cheek from where I'd punched him.

"I'm sorry."

He clasped my wrist, amusement hinting at his lips, softening the sternness that had been there only a few moments earlier.

"No, you're not. You would have clocked me a second time, if I wasn't expecting it."

I shrugged. There was no point in denying it.

"Do you really think I'm not clean?"

There was hurt underlying his words that I couldn't ignore.

I wanted to say yes but that was the jealous part of me who hated every woman he'd been with since we'd broken up. He'd been religious about protection with me, even after our wedding. I highly doubted he'd ever change in that regard.

"No. It was just hard to hear that you had a harem, because I knew you'd slept with the women here. So, I channeled that into something that would keep up our act."

"You definitely managed that."

"How many women have you bought?"

"From Trevolo?" He paused, taking a breath. "Ten. From others, more."

I swallowed.

"You sleep with all of them?"

"It's part of Julian Bonaparte's life. He likes women."

I frowned.

"I can't change what I did. You know the job as well as I do."

He was right. Many an agent had to take on their cover to the point where their real-life persona no longer existed.

Hell, I'd done such a good job at being Anastasia that Anaya hadn't made an appearance in over six months.

Adrian set my hand over his chest.

"I would give anything for it to be Anaya and Adrian again, but we have to keep up the cover. I am going to be every bit the fucked-up bastard the people on this island believe me to be.

"When I tell you to do something and you don't move fast enough, I will punish you. When others want something from you, you will always defer to me. I am the law you'll obey. You're about to see a side of me that you've never known."

"I know the background of your cover," I said.

"Ana, those men out there are the worst of the worst, and I'm the boogeyman they fear. The illusion of power and ruthlessness is as effective as killing a man. There is a chance I will have to resort to the latter."

His words had a chill going down my spine.

Instead of focusing on his last statement, I asked, "What are you going to make me do?"

He kissed my forehead. "I'm about to show you what the life of a slave is. If I tell you too much, you won't react the way I need you to. Just know, everything you see and experience for the next two weeks is to get us out of here. Trevolo cannot catch on to who we are. He's the one we need to fear. He is dangerous, and his network is long and deep. This is the closest I've gotten to being on the inside."

I swallowed, blowing out a long breath. "As long as Ian is still there when this is over, I can handle it."

"I pray to God that you can." He offered me his hand.

I slid my palm over his and he immediately drew it to his lips, kissing my knuckles.

Just as fast, he released my fingers and moved to the door. "Time to put on the performance of our lives."

CHAPTER NINE

Anaya

Adrian and I entered a large outdoor living area where a group of men sat in lounge chairs with their women...slaves kneeling on the floor next to them. One of the girls looked so young, maybe fourteen at most. I felt my stomach roll, even though I hadn't eaten anything since yesterday.

I knew this life was temporary—well, if I made it through the next couple of weeks, but for her, it was a life sentence.

Adrian abruptly came to a stop, positioning his body so I was behind him.

"Trevolo. A word."

Nodding, Trevolo approached. "What troubles you?"

"Did I not make it clear, if I am present no one is to even think about bringing in a child who cannot give consent?"

"I thought you'd make an exception for this one. She's sixteen and a personal slave accompanying Mr. Cruise."

My foot, she was sixteen. I eyed the knife sitting on a nearby table where the men had recently had breakfast.

"She is of age," a portly old man said, caressing the girl's hair. Her eyes were full of fear. As if contradicting her master would result in a severe punishment.

Something told me she was purchased at one of Trevolo's past special auctions. I couldn't believe Cruise, or whatever his name was, thought to pass off the child as consenting.

Seeing her solidified my resolve to find the bastards involved in this ring of traffickers.

"Stay here," Adrian said to me as he stalked over to the fat man and punched him in the face. The little girl shrieked as blood hit her shoulder and hair.

The man gurgled, clutching his nose. Adrian grabbed him by the throat, cutting off his air.

"You will leave this island, and never come back. If you even think about it, I will hunt you down and exterminate you. As of this moment, you have no business with me, Trevolo, or any on this island."

Adrian stared down all the men watching the scene unfold.

"If I learn any of you have any financial dealings with this scum, I will take personal interest in taking apart each and every one of your empires." Adrian turned his attention back to the man. "You will leave this island in the next fifteen minutes. Come back, and I will finish what I started."

"She's my slave," the bleeding man wheezed out.

Instead of responding, Adrian continued to squeeze until the man passed out and then threw him to the floor.

It took me a second to register what had just happened. Adrian had just done the next thing to carrying out the execution I was envisioning.

Holy fuck.

"No exceptions, ever." Adrian turned to Trevolo. "Is that clear? Or I will take my money and skills elsewhere."

Trevolo clenched his jaw, anger coloring his gaze.

That was when I remembered Ele saying enemies worked together for mutually beneficial prospects. Trevolo truly hated Adrian...no, *Julian Bonaparte*, but needed him.

I had no doubt Trevolo would get rid of Adrian immediately, given the opportunity.

Walking back to me, Adrian reached behind me to the table, grabbed a napkin, and wiped his hands.

"Follow me, Bride. Let's have breakfast while this mess is cleaned up."

I glanced toward the girl, who was sobbing into her blood-covered hands.

"She is now mine. Have her sent to my home in Cyprus. I'll decide where she goes from there."

I felt as if I were in a haze for the next hour. It was like Adrian hadn't all but killed a man in front of at least thirty people. No one seemed fazed.

Well, that wasn't true. Some of the men seemed to avoid any contact with Adrian. As if they were worried about being on his radar.

Even the island staff seemed unfazed. They moved about, serving the guests and making sure everyone was comfortable.

After a small meal, I spent time sitting uncomfortably on my tender bottom in a corner with the women of the harem.

None of us spoke, just waited to be summoned. They all seemed so calm, so seasoned. The women were of every shape and size. The only common thing was their clothes. Gowns of every shade of bright color and bodies adorned with jewels that looked real, not costume. Each was beautiful and seemed well cared for, no visible bruises or injuries. They were the pampered princesses who traded their bodies for a life of luxury. I couldn't fault them for their decisions. I had no idea what they came from.

But these women were here by choice. I had to find the

ones who were not, the ones who were hidden away in the bowels of this island. Wherever the fuck that was.

One of the women stared at me as if trying to figure me out. On occasion she'd glance at Adrian and then back at me while frowning.

I wanted to ask her what her problem was but kept my mouth shut, knowing it was better I stay silent.

"Anastasia, come here."

I snapped out of my thoughts and looked toward the group to my left. Adrian held my gaze and lifted a brow.

"Anastasia." There was a warning in his tone that had me moving toward him.

Releasing a breath, I slid onto his lap. I tried to ease down, making sure I didn't jar my aching ass.

I gasped as a possessive hand went around my waist, pulling me back. I gripped his leg, knowing if he let go, I'd fall.

"Sore?"

I nodded. The men continued to watch us with curiosity and that sick hint of lust that had been on their faces from the first time I saw them.

"Then don't misbehave. You smack me, I smack back."

I shifted, trying to get some comfort, and immediately felt Adrian's cock begin to grow and the muscles of his thighs bunch.

My heartbeat accelerated.

"Now, where were we, gentlemen?" Adrian asked.

The men began a lively discussion about trade and buyers, that I figured out referenced arms deals. I mentally began keeping notes about the locations they mentioned.

Thank God for my photographic memory. When I was debriefed after leaving this godforsaken island, I'd be able to give every last detail of what I'd heard and seen.

As the conversation continued for the next fifteen minutes, there was one man in particular who seemed to want to impress Adrian. Mica was his name. He had a large bruise marring his neck that almost looked like the imprint of tip of a man's shoe.

Adrian leaned down and whispered in my ear, "Stay very still. Don't come unless I give you permission."

"What?"

"You heard me."

Adrian picked up his tumbler, took a sip, then set it down on a nearby side table, circling the rim of the glass. He slid the hand from around my waist to under my dress. His arm was covered by my gown, but anyone watching would know what he was doing.

I stiffened, wanting desperately to shove his hand away, but knowing he'd have to discipline me in front of the group if I went with my instincts.

Adrian gripped my knee and pulled my legs slightly apart, making room for him.

Thank God the gown covered me. Well, sort of.

Adrian grazed my slit and hummed. His cum coated

his fingers from our earlier library fucking. His cock grew thick and long, sending a shiver down my spine.

He liked the feel of his semen on me. He rubbed up and down, not touching my clit or the entrance to my pussy.

My cheeks heated as did the rest of my body.

Adrian continued to chat, discussing various properties and locations of warehouses. All the while, his fingers stroked up and down my sex. Arousal and need burned my insides.

Biting my lip, I stifled a moan. My pussy quivered, and desire soaked his evil hand.

"Shh," he whispered so only I heard. "Not until I say."

A sheen of sweat dampened my body.

He pushed a finger inside me and curved up, teasing the bundle of nerves deep inside.

I dug my nails into his fabric-covered legs, trying to hold in the orgasm about to overtake me.

Adrian seemed unaffected and continued teasing me, now plunging in and out, not caring that everyone around us had grown silent as they watched us.

Adrian's other hand moved over my breast, cupping it and then pinching the tip through my dress.

I cried out, unable to control my body's response.

"Come. Let everyone know that I own this cunt." Adrian thrust deep while his thumb rubbed my clit.

I threw my head back against his chest, arched into his touch, and came.

"Oh, oh, yes."

My pussy clamped down, contracting around Adrian's pistoning finger. I lost myself in the sensation of the orgasm he'd denied me earlier.

Breathing heavily, I came back to reality and opened eyes that I hadn't realized I'd closed. Adrian withdrew from my still-quivering pussy and brought his fingers to my lips.

"Suck."

I parted my lips, sucking his digits into my mouth. My own essence mixed with his cum was a spiced blend I hadn't tasted in five years.

"Like it?"

Without thinking, I nodded.

This was so fucked up. I could feel the eyes of the men on me and couldn't care less. I was enthralled by Adrian and this connection we'd had from the beginning. Well, from the time our relationship had moved from a teenage crush to a passion that had left me scarred when it had ended.

"Good, it's something you're about to get very used to." Adrian cupped my jaw, kissing me hard before shifting his attention from me to the group around us. "This, gentlemen, is how you turn a hellcat into a dove. Force and discipline are a measure of last resort and only to convey a point."

Adrian stiffened as a man approached and said in a deep, slightly German-accented voice I somehow recognized, "Looks like I arrived a few minutes too late."

CHAPTER TEN

Anaya

My heartbeat accelerated as the man I'd known as Sebastian Kohl came into view.

Sebastian looked like he'd stepped off the pages of a mafia romance novel, with his tailored black pants and white shirt rolled up at the sleeves exposing the tattoos covering his arms. He carried himself with an edge that said he was dangerous if pushed too far. He'd definitely changed in the five years since I saw him last.

He was a tech genius like Adrian, but he knew how to let loose and had the ability to get Adrian to step away from his computers for a night out.

It looked like Sebastian had gotten Adrian to do a lot

more than go to the clubs for a night. Or maybe it was the other way around.

"I see you stole the prize before I could get here." His gaze perused my body from head to toe and then moved to Adrian.

Adrian's hand moved back around my waist, tightened for a second, and then relaxed as I leaned back against him.

"I don't waste time when I want something. Whose fault is it that you're late?"

The hostility in Adrian's voice told me Sebastian was the "Sebastian Weber" Ele was telling me about. The enemy who shared women with Adrian.

"You know as well as I do the obligations family puts on our time."

"I take it this has to do with the shipments out of the Middle East?"

"All you need to know is that it is settled." Sebastian stopped when he was in front of Adrian and me. He took my hand, brought it to his lips, and kissed the skin of my inner wrist. "Hello, beautiful."

A tingle shot into my core.

Why the fuck did his touch give me goosebumps?

It must be the endorphins left over from my orgasm.

Or the fact you were always attracted to him. He was hot back in the day and more so now.

I remained quiet and glanced at Adrian since he wanted me to defer to him when anyone spoke to me.

He inclined his head.

"Hello."

Sebastian rubbed the skin on the outside of my hand with his thumb before releasing it.

"I call dibs on being your third."

My stomach fluttered. I knew part of the whole bride thing was sharing her, but being shared was something I was hoping wouldn't happen.

However, with the heat of Sebastian's gaze and the way it affected me, I wasn't so resistant to the idea.

"We'll see." Adrian's fingers flexed on my abdomen, snapping me from my crazy thoughts. I was really losing it.

"You'll have to get in line, Weber," the man named Mica Chance said.

Both Adrian and Sebastian ignored him as they seemed to share some kind of communication only the two of them understood.

"Welcome, *Herr* Weber. How is life in Berlin?"

Sebastian turned to Trevolo, offering his hand for a shake. "As well as it can be. *Vater* sends his regards."

"Next time you should bring him."

"You know as well as I do he doesn't care for our form of sport."

"Yes, that is true. That means more for men like us. Wouldn't you agree, Bonaparte?" There was a cold, almost calculating edge to Trevolo's tone that made me think it was some sort of dig at Adrian.

"As long as it isn't with children, I'm in complete agreement." Adrian stroked his fingers up and down my arm.

"Yes. We know your preferences. Mr. Cruise was an oversight I won't make again."

"Tell us, Bonaparte, when will you choose your third?" Sebastian spoke, drawing Trevolo's attention to a different subject. Me.

"Soon," was all Adrian said, but his demeanor was hostile.

"Understandably, Mr. Bonaparte is protective of his pet. One doesn't pay twenty million and let anyone taste her," another man, referred to as Silas Finn, said with a thick Irish accent.

"Twenty million. That's interesting." Sebastian shook his head. "If you'd waited one day for the auction, I would have happily paid more."

"Then perhaps I can suggest a consolation." Trevolo approached the area where Adrian and I sat. "Especially since Mr. Bonaparte disposed of a guest before I was able to finish my business with him."

"I'm intrigued." Sebastian scanned me again and lingered on the way Adrian held me against him. "I read her report. She is definitely a unique item."

"Out of the question." Adrian's command was absolute. "I choose the man."

"You owe me, Bonaparte. An auction for who gets to be

your third is in order. Besides, it isn't as if you haven't shared a woman a time or two with Weber or even some of our other guests."

I could almost hear Adrian grind his teeth, and the thought of an auction deciding who Adrian shared me with made my stomach hurt.

Expecting Adrian to protect me with some type of edict or the other, I couldn't help my surprise when he said, "I get half of whatever you take in, and it will happen in my private bungalow on the beach. It's only fair compensation for sharing my twenty-million-dollar prize."

I started to fidget, feeling panic bubble up.

Adrian's hold tightened, almost painfully. "Quiet."

"Your bride disagrees with your choice." Sebastian smirked.

"She has no say in what I do with her." Adrian narrowed his gaze on mine, telling me to stay still without words. "Are my terms acceptable, Trevolo?"

"Accepted with one caveat," Trevolo added. "You will install a camera so we may watch and verify delivery of purchase."

"Only for the duration of the scene. Afterward, I get my privacy." Adrian waited for Trevolo to respond.

After a long pause, Trevolo said, "Done."

"Please don't do this," I said.

"Ana, quiet." Adrian stared at Sebastian. "Begin the auction, Trevolo."

"Follow me, gentlemen. I will inform Mr. Bonaparte of the winner once we are finished."

All the men who'd watched as Adrian fucked me stood, moving into a room Trevolo entered. The last to go in was Sebastian. He had a lazy pace about him that made it seem as if the results were just a formality.

The door clicked shut behind him and I turned a death glare in Adrian's direction and slapped him. I wanted to do so much more.

I'd signed up for this, but the reality of it was overwhelming. I'd been with one man in my life and it was Adrian.

The room grew quiet, with all the eyes of the remaining guests and the women scattered around the room moving to us.

"I warned you, Ana." Anger flashed over his face. "You will learn that I hit back."

A drian

I rose, throwing Ana over my shoulder, smacking her ass hard enough to make her yelp and sting my palm, and stalked down the hallway to the bridal suite.

Why the fuck did she slap me?

I'd goddamn told her I'd have to behave differently here.

She pounded on my back, saying swear words in three languages I could recognize—Italian, Hindi, and English.

The second I entered the room I dropped her to the floor and slammed the door closed.

Ana shifted as if she was about to dart for the balcony, making me growl. "Don't even think about scrambling away. I will catch you, and the punishment will be vicious and hard."

I ran a frustrated hand through my hair.

"I won't do it. I won't let you turn me into a whore."

Was this part of the role or was this how she felt? The whole situation was so fucked up.

The last thing I wanted to do was share her with any man, much less some piece of shit who won an auction. If Sebastian won, even the thought of my best friend with Ana annoyed me.

We'd shared plenty of women before, but all of them knew the game and none of them were Anaya Anthony, my woman. My fucking everything.

I paced, knowing I'd had no choice, knowing refusing would have made Julian Bonaparte look weak, would have destroyed the reputation of the asshole I had spent years to become.

"You don't get a say in what I do with you. And let's get something straight. You *are* a whore. Mine."

As angry tears clouded her vision, Ana bit out, "Why would you do this?"

"Because I can. Now come here and kneel."

As much as this was for show, I needed to feel her, to have a part of her before another man got what belonged to me.

I knew it was sick as fuck to want a blowjob to ease my tension, but it was the only thing I could think of to calm my ass down.

"You can't be serious."

"Ana, move." My words came out hard. Hard enough to get her to move until she was kneeling in front of me.

I opened my pants with only enough room to pull out my cock. Fisting the base, I pumped up and down a few times.

Her gaze went to the bead of precum at the tip of the angry head of my dick. She gave a scandalized whimper, but the way her eyes clouded with desire and she licked her lips said the opposite.

I nudged her, letting my precum coat her lips.

"Open."

A crease formed between her brows as she glared at me with her amber gaze.

Why did her defiance arouse me?

I cupped the back of her neck, applying enough pressure to get her to comply.

Pushing into her mouth, I released a groan. "Work my cock. Don't disappoint me."

God, there was truly nothing like the way this woman made me feel.

She fisted the base of my cock and pumped up and down with the movement of her delicious tongue.

"Yes." The hoarseness in my voice was unable to hide my arousal. This woman knew how to work my dick. "Take it all."

She gagged a few times and the sick-fuck side of me loved to hear the sound. I owned this mouth, hell, I owned every part of her—her cunt, her tits, her ass. God, I'd loved pushing into her precious puckered rosebud last night. The woman was made for me.

She bobbed up and down, sucking me off like it was her favorite thing to do.

She may be the one on her knees, but she knew as well as I did that she was the one with all the power.

"Ease up. I'm not ready to come." I clenched my teeth, trying desperately to hold off my orgasm.

My words spurred her to go in harder, flicking her wicked tongue in the way I liked.

"Look at me."

When she complied, I said, "I own you, Ana. I do what

I want with your body. I will share you and you will comply."

She couldn't answer and I wasn't looking for one. She held my stare as her eyes watered with each thrust of my hips.

What I wanted to ask her was if she really thought I wanted to share her, to let another man know the heaven that was her body.

"Touch yourself. Play with that pussy."

The fingers of one of her hands pumped my cock as the other worked her clit.

I smelled her need mixing with mine. It was a heady mix. I wasn't sure how I'd lived without it for all these past years.

My balls drew up and my grip in her hair grew harder. "You're mine, Ana. You were born to be mine. I won't let any other man take you from me."

She moaned, stroking the vein on the underside of my cock as I hit the back of her throat.

"Take every drop."

I exploded, spurts of cum shooting in the rhythm of my hips. Ana swallowed and swallowed. Tears streamed down her cheeks, but she never looked away from me.

She was a fucking goddess.

And I hoped to holy hell I didn't kill the man who'd get to experience her.

I pulled free of her mouth, dropping to my knees and

pushing her back. Lifting her skirt, I attacked her pussy, sucking, licking, circling.

She clutched my head and cried out, "Oh God."

Her desire soaked my face and I couldn't help but revel in her taste.

I pushed her addictive essence toward her rosebud.

"God. I'm going to come if you do that."

Instead of responding, I pushed my thumb through the tight puckered opening. She detonated, crying out and biting her fist, while the other gripped my hair.

"It's too much. It's too much. Don't stop. Don't stop."

I worked her until the last of her orgasm ebbed its way out of her.

As her grip loosened, I climbed over her body, caging her head with my arms. My cock bobbed between us, hard again from seeing her come.

We stared at each other, feeling the intensity of the situation we had no choice but to participate in.

Leaning down, I kissed her, not caring that I could taste myself. This was my woman and once this fucked ordeal was over, I was marrying her again. Consequences be damned.

Ana grabbed my erection, positioned it at her entrance, and lifted up to impale herself on my length.

I arched forward and rubbed my pelvis against her clit. Her pussy quivered and flooded with another wave of need.

"Fuck me hard. Like no man could ever fuck me and make me want more."

That one statement had me losing any semblance of control or rational thought. I began to fuck her, rut into her, pound the cunt that had only ever known my cock.

"More. Harder." Her demands were almost inaudible as she thrashed and clawed at my back.

I obliged, and we were taken away by mutual need.

When we came, it was raw, unfiltered, and filled with so much more emotion than a place like this should ever bring forth.

CHAPTER ELEVEN

Anaya

I released a deep breath as Adrian lifted his head from my shoulder and stared down at me.

We were both reeling from the intensity of our orgasms and the unsaid things between us.

This was our assignment, something that went into action without our control, but it was also us. The couple who loved so hard that it had made no sense when it had ended.

"We need to clean up. They will be here soon." He pulled out of me, making me gasp from the sudden emptiness.

Almost as if on cue, a knock came at the door.

"Go into the bathroom and wait until I come get you."

I nodded and rose to my feet. I knew my emotions were on my face. With anyone else I had no trouble masking them, pretending I felt nothing. But Adrian saw right through me. To the point where he had this crazy way of knowing what I was feeling and thinking.

I went into the bathroom, leaving the door open as Adrian straightened his clothes and answered the door.

He spoke to a messenger, but I couldn't clearly make out what was said. All I heard was the bidding was over.

The door closed and I walked back into the room.

"Do you know who won the auction?"

"Why can't you ever do a damn thing I say?" Adrian snapped.

He strode toward me, grabbing my hand, and pulled me into the bathroom. Closing the door, he shoved me back against the nearest wall, pressing his body to mine.

"You will not leave this suite unless Ele or I come to get you. I will not risk anything happening to you."

"I'm not weak."

"I know this, but they don't." He dropped his forehead to mine. "Ana, please, don't fight me on this."

I understood what he was saying. It was so hard for me to remember I wasn't Anaya with Adrian and I couldn't react to him as I normally would.

I blew out a sigh and nodded.

"Thank you." He gave me a deep kiss that I felt all the

way to my toes and stepped back. "When we get to my bungalow tonight, we have some things to discuss."

Before I could respond, he opened the door and strode out.

A n hour later, I was still waiting for news.

Pacing hadn't helped with the uneasiness I felt, so I walked out onto the balcony and leaned against the railing. Along the shore, workers busied themselves with removing seaweed that had washed up onto the sand to keep the beaches pristine. A couple walked near the cliffs. From the color of the gown, I recognized the woman as the one who couldn't keep her eyes off me in the lounge. She was holding hands with Silas Finn.

They looked like a happy couple on vacation taking a leisurely stroll. They made a striking pair. Maybe Silas would get to take her away from this place. The gentle way he touched her made me believe he'd take care of her for the rest of her life.

Damn Adrian and his sexual prowess. He'd fucked the brain cells right out of my head.

If I was this messed up now, what would I be like after two weeks of this?

An image of Adrian and me back in Vegas flashed in

my mind, of him dominating and worshiping me at the same time.

My core clenched.

Stop thinking about sex, Anaya!

At that moment, my nerves fired, and I knew someone was in the room. The door hadn't clicked to alert me, but I'd felt it.

This was the exact sensation I'd always gotten when I knew I was in danger.

I inhaled deep and waited, keeping my gaze trained in front of me. Adrian or Ele would have announced themselves.

"Hello, Anastasia. It's a wonder you're able to stand after the way Bonaparte fucked you on the floor earlier."

I turned to find Mica Chance leaning against the balcony doorframe.

"It looks like you enjoy it hard and rough. Good thing I like it the same way."

"You aren't supposed to be in here."

"I do what I want. Neither Trevolo nor Bonaparte can say anything. Your master owes me for this." He pointed to the bruising around his throat. "Turn around. A taste of his Aphrodite will suffice as payment."

The bastard was going to get a lot more than he bargained for.

I shook my head, and he clicked open a folding switchblade.

I was going to jam that knife in his face.

I gripped the railing behind me and watched Mica approach.

"I said, turn around, and if you make a sound, I will destroy this face that seems to make the men on the island spend so much money."

"P-please don't." I added a tremor to my voice. "Master Julian will be here soon."

"You should worry about me." With a quick flick of the knife, he tore the straps of my sleeveless gown, exposing my breasts.

"No." I covered my chest with my arms.

He gripped my side, digging his fingers deep, making me cry out.

"This is only the beginning." He roughly turned me, forcing me to face the water while he ground his erection against my ass.

"No," I whimpered and let tears stream down my cheeks. "Don't do this."

"I like it when they cry." He nicked my neck, drawing blood. "I like blood too."

This motherfucker was going down.

He began to lift my dress and before he moved past my thighs, I used the back of my head and smashed it into his face and then made a swift shift and kicked him in the chest.

He fell back, dropping the blade and covering his nose, blood oozing through his fingers.

Rage filled his gaze as he looked up. "Now I'm going to make you beg for me to kill you."

He charged in my direction, and with a quick kick of my left foot, my toes lifted the knife. Grabbing the blade with my right hand, I stabbed it into Mica's chest a second before he reached me.

He wailed, but it seemed to do nothing to keep him from punching me on the side of my head.

Stars burst behind my eyes and I wobbled, nearly losing balance against the balcony railing. Mica lifted his fist to hit me again, but I pulled out the knife and jabbed the blade in his face.

He stumbled backward, making a gurgling sound and falling to the ground.

I gasped in air, shaking for real this time. My head hurt like nothing I'd felt before. I slid to the floor, feeling too weak to do anything else.

Dear God. I'd just killed a man.

Though the bastard deserved it for trying to rape me and who knew how many he'd succeeded with before me.

This wasn't my first kill, but there was a huge difference between taking care of someone through the scope of my sniper rifle and with my hand, up close.

I dropped my head back against the railing and

winced. A throbbing had started, and I had no doubt I had some type of concussion.

I had to stay awake, but my eyelids felt so heavy. God, I was so tired.

Where the hell was Adrian?

I lifted my hands to cover my head, but blood dripped from my fingers. Glancing at where Mica's sprawled dead body lay, a sense of dread washed over me.

How was I going to explain any of this? Would there be some consequences? Had I just compromised the whole operation?

Dizziness began to overwhelm me, as did nausea.

Fuck. Where is Adrian? Stay awake, Anaya, stay awake.

But it was no use. I had to close my eyes.

Adrian

"Ana, baby wake up," I said in a whisper to a sleeping Anaya, for the millionth time since I'd found her covered in blood and passed out two days ago.

My heart had all but died seeing her so lifeless.

I should have stayed with her or brought her with me and none of this would have happened. No matter how strong she thought she was, Anaya was no competition for a man with at least a hundred pounds on her and no qualms with fighting dirty.

She killed him, asshole—she was strong enough.

I gripped the base of my neck.

The bruises on her face and the cut on her neck had begun to heal, and according to the doctors brought in by Trevolo, she had a concussion but no brain bleeds or permanent trauma. Sleep was the best medicine for her.

I couldn't trust the motives of any doctor on Trevolo's payroll, but I had no choice but to wait. There was no way to bring in a second opinion without compromising the investigation.

I hated waiting like this.

If the bastard Trevolo hadn't dragged out the announcement with a cocktail hour, I'd have gotten back to the room in time. He'd done it on purpose to fuck with me.

I was well aware of the procedures in an auction like the one for Ana. The men who were interested in the auction had instructions to write down the highest possible bid for a night as my third and seal it in an envelope.

All the fucker had to do was read out each cap bid and go from there.

When I noticed Chase missing, I knew something was wrong. The beady-eyed fucker hadn't kept his eyes off Ana from the moment he'd tried to touch her in her cell.

Thank God it was part of Trevolo's rules to only read

the winner in the presence of the bidders—it gave me an excuse to leave.

What I hadn't expected was a frantic Ele running into the lounge to say Chase was dead.

I knew instantly it was in my suite. Finding Ana's limp body had all but destroyed me. It had taken five men to hold me off the guards who'd left their posts for a smoke. I wanted them to suffer the same fate Chase had, and I had wanted to do it by throwing them from the third-story balcony.

The only consolation was that Trevolo had done the task for me.

The door to my bungalow opened, and I immediately knew who it was. There was only one person with the know-how to circumvent my security. Sebastian.

He appeared a few seconds later. "How is she doing?"

"Get lost, Weber."

"Trevolo wants you at the house."

"Tell him to fuck off too."

"Stop being a dick. You're lucky he let you hole up in here with her."

"I don't give a shit." I was not going to leave Ana's side until she was awake and trying to punch me again. "Why are you here, Weber?"

"As I said. To relay Trevolo's messages." He paused. "And to bring you some food."

"No, I mean, why the fuck are you on this island? Your

showing up complicated things."

Sebastian and I had received invitations to the auction at the same time but our higher-ups had decided I would be the one to go in because I had the deepest infiltration into Trevolo's world.

"No. My showing up kept Anaya's team from changing their minds and storming the island to take out everyone on it. They received word a shipment is arriving on the island in a few days, which means a special auction is imminent."

"Wouldn't that mean it is more important than ever to find out who the buyers are? What aren't you saying?"

"Ana's handler wants her off the island as soon as possible. She suspects Trevolo is going to steal Ana from you and sell her to another bidder."

That made no sense, but then again Trevolo tended to make deals and then double-cross for a side benefit.

Sebastian continued, "We're lucky they even contacted us. They put their operation on hold for ours. Her handler is one piece of work. She threatens to chop both our dicks off if we don't get her out of here before any shit goes down."

I had no doubt Briana would do it. Compared to Briana, Ana was tame. It may have to do with being in the business longer or it could just be her sunny disposition.

"Did they give a time frame for how long they'll sit back?"

"One week. Afterward, the North American director is

stepping in. She makes our directors look like teddy bears."

"Who the fuck is their North American director? A female version of Rambo?"

Sebastian laughed and slapped me on the back. "The first lady. In a technical sense, she's your new mother-in-law."

"Say that again."

"You heard me. The wife of the leader of the free world is the head of operations for Solon North America. She views all her people as family. And since Anaya was on loan for an operation in Europe, she is taking this personally."

I sat there processing. Tara Zain Kumar, the pint-sized former human-rights attorney, was a Solon agent. She had to be one of the best to earn her role, but damn.

The president was married to a spy?

I bet that went over well when he found out. Ashur Kumar was a stickler for rules and using the law to make change, and he was married to a woman who helped circumvent the law.

I just developed a newfound respect for the guy.

"Any way you can convince them to extend the time?"

"We're lucky we got what we have."

I glanced at Ana. Her color was coming back. At least that was something.

"Dammit, I wasn't there to protect her. How am I going to explain this to her family?"

"You won't. From what I get, no one knows she is anything more than a marketing, social media, and design consultant for the fashion industry." Sebastian handed me a bottle. "Drink this, and there's food in the front room. Let's talk more in there."

I took the water, twisting the cap and taking a long gulp. "I'll eat later."

"She's not going anywhere." He gestured with his head. "Eat while I fill you in on some other interesting information I learned as Trevolo's guest."

"Fine." I got up, giving Ana another scan and then pushing past Sebastian. I moved into the open area encompassing the living room and kitchen. Covered dishes sat on two oversized trays on the coffee table. Was he planning on feeding me for a week?

The bungalow was small but as secure as possible. I would know the second anyone even thought to activate a listening device or camera.

Trevolo had installed many devices over the years but regretted it when I'd relocated each one to the toilet of his guards' quarters. The man had no idea I'd been hacking since I was a child and worked with the best to learn my skills.

I sat on the couch, pulled the first tray toward me, and opened the lids on the plates. The aroma of spiced chicken wafted into the air and my stomach growled.

Guess I was hungry after all.

I took a few bites and then said, "Talk. You'll need to be out of here soon."

Sebastian rolled his eyes. "For someone who just said to tell Trevolo to fuck off, you seem worried about him."

I shot him a glare. "Stop stalling, asshole."

"He knows Ana isn't Anastasia Ashton."

I looked up from my plate. "How?"

"He suspected it, ever since his bitch wife had a meltdown at a fitting and wanted him to keep an eye on Ana. He thinks she's Nora, the runaway daughter of Sharibin Shah."

Sharibin Shah was an Indian industrialist who ran his organization and family with an iron hand. He was also a well-known drug and arms trafficker. There were rumors Shah had muscled Trevolo out of a lucrative deal a time or two.

"That's a stretch. Ana doesn't have anything to do with that family."

"It's the eyes. How many people do you know that have the same amber, tiger-like color? She also looks eerily similar to the daughter that ran away from a supposed arranged marriage."

I digested this. "So not only was she taken because of my interest in her, but because she resembled a rival's daughter?"

"Yes and no. Catarina Trevolo's jealousy was the cause of Ana being noticed in the first place. The fact she resembled the type of Indian women you gravitated toward in the harem gave him a business opportunity and a reason to justify his taking her. The rival's-daughter thing just turned out to be a bonus."

I waited, knowing I wasn't going to like what he was about to add.

"Take a good look at the last known picture of Nora Shah."

Sebastian set his phone on the table next to the tray. There was no doubt in my mind that Nora Shah was Anaya Anthony. The hair color and style of clothing were nearly the same as Ana's real-life persona.

I clenched my teeth. "I swear as soon as she wakes up, I'm going to paddle her ass."

"You're not the only one with multiple fake lives. According to Ana's handler, she is one of the best at blending into her roles, though most of the time she hides her eyes with contacts."

"Since when did you have time to make friends with a Solon agent, especially Briana Amici?"

He lifted a brow and smirked. "I should have expected you to know Bri. And to answer your question, I have worked with Bri on multiple cases over the years. You have to remember, I'm Interpol and German, not American CIA. We tend to make more friends than enemies when working with other agencies to reach our end goal."

"Fuck off."

"We have more problems to add to everything."

"You are just full of good news today." I took a deep breath. "Spit it out."

"There is no way Trevolo is going to believe she is an ordinary capture, daughter of a rival or not."

"What the hell are you talking about?"

"You saw the video just as everyone else did. Only someone who is trained in combat would know how to make the moves Ana made. Trevolo isn't an idiot. Plus, the way she kicked up that blade and stabbed Chase was some serious James Bond shit."

"Lara Croft," Ana's weak, hoarse voice said. "Or Selene from *Underworld*. You could pick a female badass to describe me, not some stupid British Secret Service agent."

She leaned heavily against the door leading out of the bedroom. Her face was flushed, and she gripped her side in the spot with some of her worst bruising.

I rushed to her, scooping her into my arms.

"I'd lean more toward Selene. She is a German death dealer, after all. We Germans are very badass."

I shot Sebastian an annoyed glare and cradled Ana's head against my neck. "You scared the shit out of me."

"I'm sorry." She nuzzled into me. "I scared myself too."

I brought her to the couch and sat, keeping her on my lap. I closed my eyes and said a quick prayer of thanks and then leaned back.

I was not letting her out of my sight from now on. Damn woman got into trouble even when she was doing as she was told. Her safety was virtually nonexistent on this godforsaken island.

"I want to get her off this island as soon as possible. Use your connections or something. Right now, you're Trevolo's favorite lapdog."

"I am no one's lapdog." The humor on Sebastian's face disappeared. "Trevolo is going to have Ana and you watched nonstop the second he learns she's awake. The only way to keep her safe is to play our assigned roles."

"The bastard is going to expect me to share her. Whether she's recovered or not. It's fucking out of the question."

"Do you really believe I would hurt her? You're lucky I scare the shit out of the others as much as you do and no one challenged my bid."

"Are you boys really discussing me as if I'm not here?" Ana shifted, trying to sit up, but I held her down.

"Dammit. Stay still—you have a fucking head injury. I won't let you get hurt again."

She jabbed me with her elbow in the gut and slid from my hold, cocking a hand on her hip.

"Fuck. What was that for?"

"Do you see this?" She pulled down the shoulder of my too-big-for-her shirt and exposed the small, jagged scar marring her shoulder. "I went back to work within days of this."

I clenched my jaw. She'd been shot. She shouldn't be out in the field, she should be back in Vegas, running her family's empire.

"I highly suggest that if you don't want to die, you stop that line of thought." Sebastian grabbed Ana's wrist a second before she landed a punch to my face.

She winced from the strain. She was no way near recovered or able to handle this operation.

"Dammit, Ana." I reached for her, but she scrambled toward the other side of the couch.

"I'd refrain from touching her. You saw her Selene moves."

"Fuck off, Weber."

Fire flashed in Ana's amber gaze and my cock jumped. I should have my head checked but her temper turned me on. Always had.

Makeup-less, she looked so much younger than her twenty-six years. But no less beautiful. I resisted the urge to haul her toward me and kiss her.

"I'm not helpless, Ian. I know how this game is played." Ana's attention went to Sebastian. "Since I overheard you say you knew Briana, I assume they know what's going on here?"

"I'm not sure what you're talking about," Sebastian hedged and then when Ana glared at him, he said, "Yes, she's aware. Your whole team is. Hence the reason they set a deadline to get you off this island."

"What's the ETA?" Ana asked.

"A week."

"Okay." She inhaled deep. "So that means Trevolo will want to collect on the auction for third."

"Yes." I pushed the tray in her direction to distract her.

Immediately she picked up a fork and shoveled a bite into her mouth. We'd talk about the details later. I was positive she knew Sebastian was the winner to be my third, especially after the conversation about Sebastian hurting her.

Ana devoured the food, barely taking time to swallow. The one thing Ana never shied away from was food. She loved a good meal, and I was glad it hadn't changed.

"I have to say it's refreshing to be around a woman who likes to eat." Sebastian offered her a bottle of water. "Probably accounts for your fabulous curves."

I had the distinct urge to punch Sebastian. He'd said that on purpose to piss me off.

It used to annoy me the way he'd flirt with her when we were in college; however, I'd let it go because Ana seemed oblivious. Now it was a different story. He was going to get a taste of what was mine.

"Thanks." Ana shot a look between me and Sebastian and shook her head. "That's the one positive of this damn island. The chef is top notch."

Sebastian's watch beeped. "That's my cue to head back to the main house. One question before I leave?"

I lifted a brow and waited.

"How do you suppose we spin your badass Lycan slayer abilities?"

"Easy," Ana said, in between bites. "Nora Shah is an avid supporter of mixed martial arts and trains on the regular with some of the best in the world. Her father believed each of his children should learn some type of extracurricular activity. So instead of something acceptable to elitist Indian society like piano or sewing, she picked taekwondo. If Trevolo investigated Nora thoroughly enough, as we should assume he has, then it shouldn't surprise him that I have the abilities I do."

Both Sebastian and I stared at Ana as if we were seeing a different woman. Then Sebastian broke the silence with a booming laugh. "Damn, Ana, you really have all the answers." Sebastian looked at me. "You better marry her before I steal her from you."

"Don't make me kill you, Weber. Get out. I want to be alone with my bride."

The smirk on his face said he was fucking with me. If he wasn't my best friend, I'd rearrange his face.

Sebastian rose, moving to the door. "See you at the house later. Trevolo mentioned something about special entertainment. It should be interesting."

CHAPTER TWELVE

Anaya

Adrian remained quiet for a few minutes after Sebastian left, seemingly lost in thought and giving me enough time to finish eating.

"Are you okay?" I asked when I couldn't take the silence anymore.

"Yes."

"So, I take it Sebastian won the auction."

"Caught that, did you?"

I'd caught a lot of things. He'd been so lost in his discussion about me that he hadn't even noticed I had heard the majority of his conversation with Sebastian.

A slight crease formed between his brows.

"Are you going to be okay with it?"

He didn't answer and asked, "Are you okay with it?"

"I don't have a choice." Two could play this evasion game.

He glared at me. "It will only be one time."

"You've shared women before."

It made me a little crazy, knowing he was expert on this threesome thing. How many women had he shared with Sebastian or another man? Was I really looking for an answer? No. Definitely not.

"They weren't you." He turned. "I'll be right back, finish eating."

Okay, great conversation. I set my fork on the plate and stood. A wave of dizziness hit me but calmed just as fast. I padded my way into the bedroom to hear the water running in the bathroom.

The scent of lavender hit my nose and I realized Adrian was drawing me a bath.

As I stepped into the bathroom, I found Adrian holding the edge of the counter near the sink. His head was bowed and his eyes closed.

I stepped behind him, slipping my hands around his stomach and startling him.

"How the hell do you do that? You're the only person who can sneak up on me." He turned, catching me around the waist and pulling me against him.

I dropped my head to his chest, inhaling his comforting scent. "Years of practice."

"Ready for a bath?"

"God yes." I hadn't realized how cruddy my body felt until he asked the question.

"Then let's get you in there." Immediately he slipped his shirt over my head and threw it on the floor.

He clenched his jaw as he studied the bruises on my face.

Cupping his cheek, I said, "I bruise easily. You've always known this. They fade just as fast."

"I wasn't there to protect you."

"This isn't your fault."

"On that matter, we'll agree to disagree." He walked me toward the tub. "Step in."

With Adrian's help, I climbed into the giant jacuzzi that could fit five people with bubbles almost overflowing the rim.

As I settled in, I picked up a cup sitting on the ledge and poured heated water over my head and face. Slowly the heat seeped into my skin and my muscles began to relax.

"Aren't you getting in with me?"

"Are you sure you want me to?"

That was a dumb question, but I knew he was filled with guilt for what happened. The man had no idea this wasn't the first time I'd had my ass kicked. I'd keep that bit of information to myself or he may have an aneurysm.

I handed him a shampoo bottle. "Get in and wash my hair for me."

He watched me as if weighing whether to obey.

I lifted a brow and shook the bottle. "I'm waiting."

He heaved a deep sigh and pulled his shirt over his head. "Stubborn woman."

Holy fuck, the man really was the stuff of fantasies or hot cop calendars.

"Stop looking at me like that. I'm not going to do anything but help you bathe." His pants went next. God, I loved how he always went commando. He wasn't aroused by any means, but his cock was still a sight to behold. If only I had the energy to wake it up. With my mouth.

"Scoot up."

He stepped in behind me, setting a leg on each side of me and his cock resting on the curve of one butt cheek.

He washed my hair, massaging my scalp and rinsing it. He really had magic hands.

Picking up a nearby washcloth, he poured some soap on it and began to wash my body. By the time he was done, my nipples beaded and clit swelled.

My breath was coming out in short pants.

Adrian's cock responded to the change in my breathing, growing hard and thick along my spine.

"Ian," I moaned.

He set the washcloth on the side and gripped the edge of the tub, dropping his head back.

"I'm not going to fuck you until you're healed."

"Please."

"Ana, I can't hurt you."

It was crazy. He'd spank me, dominate me, fuck me every which way possible but the possibility of intentionally inflicting unnecessary pain on me was unbearable to him.

"Fine." I leaned back against his chest, making sure the length of his cock slid between my folds.

His hands grabbed my hips, staying me. "Stop it."

"Ian, please." I grabbed one of the hands on my hips and pressed it between my legs. "I need you."

"Ana, you don't understand. I'll hurt you. I don't have the ability to go gentle." His fingers began to trail up and down my slit.

"I'm not fragile." I lifted up and impaled myself on his fingers and gasped.

"Dammit, Ana." He pulled out and plunged back in. "I'll pleasure you, but my cock stays where it is."

"Between my legs."

"Ana." His tone was warning me but he continued to work my pussy, thrusting in and out as his thumb circled and teased my clit.

I gripped the back of his neck, arching up so I could grab his hot, hard length with my other hand.

"Fuck. Yes. Like that." He bucked up into my hold.

I pumped him in time to the rhythm between my legs.

"Come, Ana. Come for me."

As if on command, my body clenched down, ecstasy clouding my mind. My pussy contracted in hard ripples, leaving me lost in pleasure.

When I finally came down, I realized my fingers still held Adrian's cock and his breathing was erratic.

"I'm so going to paddle your ass for this."

"You do realize that completely goes against what you said earlier about hurting me."

"There is a difference. When I paddle you, it ends with you coming all over my cock."

"I can't argue with that."

A drian

A na and I arrived in the main house a little before nine in the evening. I'd avoided the formal dinner on purpose, knowing Trevolo would try to use it as a way to separate me from Ana. His house rules said slaves dined with other slaves. I wasn't going to have anyone else thinking they could touch her. No matter how well she'd defended herself, her current condition would leave her completely helpless.

"Stop worrying."

"Ana, don't defy me. Remember, you're my slave. Don't let anyone think you feel more for me than as your master."

"What makes you think I feel anything at all?"

I glared at her. "Because I know you better than any other person on this earth."

"Whatever."

"Just for the record, I feel the same way about you."

She stared at me with surprise.

Before she could respond, I pulled her into the hallway leading to the lounge.

The closer we got to the room, the sounds of music and sex grew louder. The second we crossed the threshold, Ana froze. Half of the room was engaged in some form of sexual activity. Women between the legs of some of the guests, sucking their cocks, while others were being fucked in every position imaginable.

It was hedonism at its finest.

Sebastian sat at the bar, seemingly unfazed by the activities going on around him. He caught my stare and smirked, then turned to say something to the bartender.

Ana wrapped her arm around mine. "What the fuck is that?"

"Trevolo is sharing his harem of slaves for the night as a thank-you for attending the auctions."

"Did you ever participate in this?"

I remained quiet, knowing she may lose her shit if I told her the truth. A truth I was positive she'd already figured out.

"I take that as yes." Then she said in her father's native language of Gujarati, *"He was all pissed off about me sleeping with another man for my assignment and he's probably fucked most of Trevolo's harem. Men and their fucking double standards."*

It took all my effort to keep a straight face. Her outrage was comical.

My sister, Penny, was trilingual, speaking Greek, English, and her mother's tongue of Gujarati. I'd thought it unfair she could talk about me behind my back, so I took lessons. Now I was really happy I had.

"No man wants his woman sleeping with another man. Even if the woman doesn't believe she still belongs to him."

"As I said, double standard." She paused and tilted her head, realizing I'd spoken to her in Gujarati. *"Shit, I forgot you learned because you thought Penny, Henna, and I were talking about you when we were kids."*

"Are you laughing at me? I was ten—who knew what you girls were saying."

"The only person we talked about was your crazy mom."

"I didn't need to learn a new language to figure that one out."

I felt the question she wanted to ask but didn't. How

was I handling my mother and her drama? She probably didn't know that I had cut all ties with her and I had people monitoring all her communications so she kept her antics at a minimum.

"Sir. Master Trevolo asks you to join the group in the lounge." An attendant approached us and gestured for us to take the steps into the main area.

We walked past a man who groaned out his climax as he held a woman's head down on his cock.

I scanned the room and found Silas Finn in a corner with his favorite harem girl, Victoria. She was his preferred slave for every visit, and from the way she was kissing him while she rode him, I'd say the feeling was mutual.

Then I spotted Trevolo half-naked with a blonde bent over a back table as he fucked her. She was still dressed for the most part. There was a group of men near them jacking themselves off.

I guided Ana toward Sebastian, but her focus was on Trevolo. "She's his main mistress. He fucks all the women in the harem, but she is the one he prefers."

"But what about Ele?"

"She isn't someone Trevolo will share with anyone. Well, only as a last resort."

"We take Ele with us," Ana said, switching back to Gujarati.

"That's the plan," I responded and then went back to

English when we neared Sebastian. "Not interested in partaking in the fun?"

Sebastian lifted a brow. "I've bought a night with the prize. I have no need for anything else."

"I couldn't agree more. Who needs anything but the bride?" Trevolo came toward us.

He was zipping up his pants, and a server brought him a bowl to wash his hands and a towel. I glanced over his shoulder to see his mistress climb onto the cock of one of the men who'd watched her, while she took another in her mouth, and a third pressed into her ass.

She seemed to enjoy what she was doing. There was a huge difference between choosing to live this life and being forced into it.

"How long until she is recovered?" Trevolo studied Ana, lifting his hand to touch her face, but pulled back when he saw me take a step toward him. "I'd say a few more days at the most."

Ana's gaze went to me.

"Your bride is frightened." Trevolo chuckled. "She'll lose that fear soon enough."

"It seems more that she is curious." Sebastian turned in our direction and spoke. "I'm sure her master is preparing her plenty."

"Why don't the three of you get better acquainted." Trevolo gestured to an unoccupied section of the room with a few armchairs positioned in a circle.

Motherfucker. He wanted a show with her.

"She hasn't recovered yet." I kept Ana by my side.

Trevolo smirked. "There is a difference between having your slave service you and then servicing her. *Herr* Weber knows how to give her pleasure without causing her discomfort."

I wasn't going to win this fucking one. God, I hoped Ana was ready for this.

"Ana, would you care if I escorted you to your seat?" Sebastian asked, grabbing her hand.

Ana's hold on my arm grew harder, and if I didn't say something it would only give Trevolo ammunition to fuck with me.

"Go, Ana. Weber will get you more comfortable. He knows what is permissible and what isn't."

She hesitated, as Trevolo would expect.

"Ana," I warned.

She bit her lip and nodded, letting Sebastian lead her away.

"Don't look at me like that, my friend. Weber is waiting to claim his purchase to allow for her full recovery. This is the least you can do. Besides, she is the one who benefits."

I schooled my face into an emotionless mask.

"So be it. Don't pull any more of this shit. You need me and my father too much to risk me pulling our aid."

"I look at it as a mutually beneficial relationship. If it

wasn't for me, you wouldn't have your bride. It was the eyes, wasn't it? That's what drew you to her."

"Her eyes do capture a man."

"She's also a prize for another reason."

I stared down at him, waiting for him to continue.

"She is Nora Shah. She is the daughter of—"

I finished his sentence. "Sharibin Shah. I already knew this."

Surprise flashed over Trevolo's face. "Were you aware of this in Italy?"

"I suspected, but her background checked out. Then when I arrived here, I was positive."

"Now I understand the reason behind your purchase. You plan to send her back to her father used."

Sharibin Shah had a reputation for wanting his daughters kept under lock and key until he arranged advantageous matches for them. He expected his female children to remain virgins and had them followed to ensure it. A whored-out daughter would be a slap in the face and would have her lose her worth in his eyes.

I'd believed the story until I learned it was Ana's cover family. Now I was blown away at how deep Solon went to achieve their end goals.

"I'll send her back once I have consumed the purchase price from her body." I turned to look at Sebastian and Ana.

He had Ana pressed back against the sofa with her dress pushed up to her thighs. I clenched my teeth.

This is part of the game, asshole.

"I believe I will join my bride and direct the scene as I see fit."

I left Trevolo and strode toward Sebastian and Ana. Some of the men and women shifted their attention to me and where I was going, but I couldn't let anyone see I was bothered by the scene about to happen or the fact most of them would watch as Ana was touched by another man.

Ana's worried gaze went immediately to mine as I took a seat across from her and Sebastian.

"Your bride is shy," Sebastian said as he lifted the hem of her dress farther up.

"That's because she knows she's mine."

"Mind if I have a taste?"

Any other woman I would have said, "go to town," but this was Ana. My Ana.

To this date, I'd been the only man to ever touch her, taste her, fuck her.

"For her pleasure only. Do not cause her discomfort. She isn't ready for what you like."

"Understood." Sebastian trailed his fingers up Ana's arms, over her shoulders, and down the valley between her breasts.

"Ana, you don't come unless I tell you," I said. "Do I make myself clear?"

She nodded and then whimpered as Sebastian pulled down one strap of her gown and took her nipple into his mouth. She cried out as he bit the tip, digging her nails into the arms of the chair.

My cock hardened hearing her sounds of desire. This was so fucked up.

Sebastian released one perfect straining bud and repeated the process on the other. Ana arched and bit her lip. Her gorgeous face was flushed.

She held my gaze, tormented by having to go through with this act and enjoying it at the same time.

I wanted to kiss her, tell her it was okay, that Sebastian would take care of her, but I couldn't.

Sebastian released her nipple with a pop and tugged her straps back up before he moved lower.

"I've wanted to taste this cunt ever since I walked in and saw you sucking your juices from Bonaparte's fingers."

Sebastian lifted Ana's hips toward him and latched on to her pussy. She gasped and moaned, squeezing her eyes tight. Sebastian licked and sucked her clit, feasting on her. He slid a hand between her folds and pushed his thumb into her ass and a finger into her dripping cunt. In and out, in and out, he fucked her.

"Master. Help me." She cried out, and I knew she was losing herself in her need.

"Come, Ana. Show Weber what he is only going to get for one night."

Ana screamed, tossing her head side to side, riding out her orgasm as Sebastian fucked her with his mouth.

After a few moments, Sebastian pulled away, wiping his mouth on his shirt sleeve and straightening Ana's dress.

"Come here, Ana." Ana opened her eyes, still glazed by her orgasm, and rose on weak legs.

She took the hand I offered her and slid onto my lap, closing her eyes.

CHAPTER THIRTEEN

Anaya

"Turn around and get on all fours," Adrian's deep voice murmured into my ear as I woke for what seemed like the tenth time tonight.

"Ian." I moaned, feeling my arousal pooling between my legs.

How was I aroused even though I just woke up? The man was a fucking machine. He'd fucked me five times already. He couldn't possibly have any more cum left in him. He was seriously determined to mark every part of me before Sebastian joined us tomorrow night.

I heard the pop of a bottle top and my ass immediately clenched.

"Again?" I whimpered.

He'd taken me in my forbidden hole earlier tonight. Though I enjoyed it more than I wanted to admit, I wasn't sure I was up for another round. He had a big cock and my ass hadn't quite recovered from it.

"Yes. I'm making up for lost time. Your ass is a work of art and I want to bury myself in it."

I opened my mouth to protest but he flipped me on my stomach, pulling my hips back.

"Ian," I gasped and glared at him over my shoulder.

He slapped my butt cheek, hard. And instead of screaming at the sting, a moan escaped.

"You want it just as bad as I do."

I couldn't deny the truth. Being with Adrian was like having all my dirty fantasies come to life. Though this situation was the last place I wanted to live them out.

"You ready?" He smeared cool gel on my puckered entrance.

"If I say yes, will you let me sleep after?"

He rimmed the tight ring of muscle with the thick flared head of his cock. "If I said yes, I'd be lying. I plan to fuck your pussy at least one more time tonight."

"Oh, God," I said through clenched teeth as he pushed into my anal passage.

I inhaled deep, trying to relax my muscles and make it easier for him and me in turn. He worked in slow thrusts until he was in to the hilt.

Then he pushed me forward until I was lying on my stomach and his body blanketed me.

He nipped my shoulder with his teeth and at the same time pistoned in and out.

"You have no idea how many nights I've fantasized about you like this. You're mine, Ana, no matter what we do tomorrow."

He paused his thrusts and threaded his fingers with mine. "Will you forgive me for not protecting you from this?"

The onslaught of emotion in his tone had me lifting up and turning my head to look at him.

His emerald gaze was molten even in the darkness of the night.

"This isn't something either of us wants but it isn't your fault. Just know you're the only man I want. The only man I have ever wanted."

My words seemed to soothe the torment in him, and he touched his forehead to mine before kissing me and resuming his thrusts.

He released one of my hands and then slid it between the mattress and my body until he reached my clit. He strummed the bundle of nerves as he pounded his cock in and out of my ass. My pussy quickened and contracted.

My fingers curled into the sheets as the need to orgasm skyrocketed. "Yes, fuck me, Ian. Harder."

"Fuck, fuck, fuck. I can't hold out anymore. Come, baby, come with me."

A few more strokes of his finger and I lost myself to the oblivion of pleasure with Adrian following a few thrusts later.

CHAPTER FOURTEEN

Anaya

The following night, Adrian, Sebastian, and I entered the bungalow. I moved to the spot in the living room by the sofa as Adrian instructed.

My pulse beat an unsteady rhythm as anticipation mixed with desire. This was going to be so different than that first night on the island with Adrian or what Sebastian had done to me the other night.

I couldn't believe another man was going to fuck me. It didn't matter that Sebastian had already gone down on me. I was entering new territory.

My skin prickled the second the door closed. The energy in the room was charged, filled with sexual tension.

Adrian moved to a corner to place a small pin-sized object on top of a bookcase.

"Activate the feed," Sebastian said in a low whisper.

"Done," Adrian responded and strolled toward me. His eyes were a molten emerald.

Was he okay with this? Would we be able to handle the aftermath of bringing another person into our relationship, even if it was only for a night?

With a finger, Adrian tilted my face up and leaned down, biting my lower lip and giving it a slight sting.

My body instantly responded.

"Stop worrying. I know who you belong to and so do you."

I nodded as I continued to gaze up at him.

Adrian reached behind him and pulled out a deep red silk blindfold.

Where the hell had he gotten that?

I pushed the thought back. It was better I didn't know.

He covered my eyes, completely blocking out my vision, and then secured the blindfold with a knot behind my head. Immediately, my senses fired, as did a wave of anxiety. The intoxicating scent of both men permeated the room. It was like rolling in rich chocolate and cognac.

"I want you to feel, to enjoy. This will be the only time in your life you will ever get to experience what it's like to have two men worship you at the same time."

I was about to ask him if he saw a future for us, but he

squeezed my jaw. "This doesn't end here, Ana. I am the only man who will touch you for the rest of your life. You're mine."

My breath grew shallow and my lips trembled.

Sebastian stepped behind me and trailed a finger down my spine.

"Are you ready, Ana?"

I exhaled and nodded. "Yes."

The men moved closer, the heat of their bodies, their raw masculinity almost overwhelming.

Dear God. We hadn't even started and I was having a head trip.

Cupping my face, Adrian said with a bit of an edge to his voice I had never heard before, "Ana, you will do everything Weber and I say. He knows the hard limits. You will not argue. Do I make myself clear?"

"Yes."

"Good. She's all yours to satisfy." Adrian moved away. I reached out to grab hold of him, but he warned, "Ana."

A shiver shot down my spine as I pulled back and waited to see what Sebastian would do.

"Shh." Sebastian lifted my hair, set it over one shoulder, and then kissed my neck a second before he licked up to my ear.

"Ohhh," I couldn't help but moan.

"That's it, Ana. Enjoy this. Let me give you pleasure." He hooked the straps of my gown with his thumbs, pulling them down my arms and letting the gown drop to the rug. "You truly have the body of a real-life Aphrodite."

He ran his fingers up the sides of my body, over my stomach, and to the tips of my breasts. He gave my puckered nipples a firm pinch, almost on the edge of too much, and then released.

I bit my lip, holding in a cry.

"No, Ana. I want to hear every sound, every moan, every scream." He repeated the delicious torture on my sensitive buds, and this time I called out.

"Oh God." I clenched my fists at my sides, hoping I could keep my balance.

"That's it." He drifted lower, until he reached the top of my pussy lips. "Give me your hand. We need to put it to good use."

Without thinking, I obeyed, and he pushed my fingers through my soaked slit, rolling my clit.

"Too bad this beautiful pussy of yours is off limits for my cock. I would have reveled in losing myself in your tight, sweet cunt."

My legs grew weak as my pussy contracted, aching for release.

"Please, I have to come. Let me come."

Sebastian slid an arm around my waist, holding me to him, the heavy length of him molding itself to my back.

"Then come, Ana. Let go," he crooned into my ear, squeezing my clitoral nub between my fingers.

I whimpered, feeling the pressure deep inside building but unable to let go. Why the fuck couldn't I let go?

That was when I felt Adrian's presence.

"Come for us baby. It's okay." He cupped my breast and then took a tip into his mouth, as Sebastian worked my hand against my clit.

Adrian bit down on my nipple and immediately I detonated.

"Oh God, oh God, oh God." My pussy spasmed and flooded mine and Sebastian's fingers.

Adrian licked and nipped at my breast until my release ebbed and my mind came back to the present.

"She can't come without you, it seems." Sebastian slid my hand from my slit and brought it up to his lips, sucking each of my fingers until they were clean of my essence. The sucking of his lips caused a tingling sensation over my skin.

"I told you she was mine." There was a smug satisfaction to Adrian's words.

"So you did." Sebastian tugged me away from Adrian. "But for now, she is mine."

He turned me, threaded his fingers into my hair, and drew me toward him. His lips were soft, softer than I expected. He kissed me with slow tastes, not going deeper than a few passes of his mouth.

"You taste like a decadent wine. No wonder he can't get enough of you."

I couldn't respond. Sebastian's words were seducing me, making me feel things I'd only ever felt for Adrian.

He kissed me again, but this time it was more forceful, more passionate, just *more*. His tongue rolled and rubbed against mine, clouding my brain.

Wrapping my arms around his shoulders, I lost myself to the embrace, enjoying this man who wasn't mine. While the one who was watched us.

Sebastian pulled back, kissing my forehead. "You are quite extraordinary. Come with me. I want to feel that tongue of yours work my cock."

I hesitated, then heard Adrian say, "Go on, little dove. I'm not going anywhere."

I nodded and allowed Sebastian to guide me to what I assumed was the sofa.

"Kneel." Sebastian helped me onto a pillow on the floor.

Without thinking, I leaned back on my heels and set my palms over my knees.

I heard both men take in a sharp breath.

"She's fucking perfect." Sebastian rubbed his thumb over my lower lip.

"I know."

Adrian's raspy voice gave me the confidence to keep going without worry. I was positive he was aroused by what was happening.

Reaching forward, I lifted up and glided my palms up

Sebastian's pant legs. His cock lay rigid, thick, and hard along his inner thigh.

Dear God. He was as big as Adrian.

For a moment, the thought of having both men in me had a wave of panic prickling the back of my mind. This was not going to work without tearing me in half.

"We will fit," Adrian said, reading my thoughts.

How the hell did he do that?

I turned in the direction of where he sat. "I'm not so sure."

"I am." I couldn't see his expression, but I was positive there was a smirk on his beautiful face.

"Let me help you become more acquainted with my cock. It may help you worry less."

Sebastian freed his erection, wrapping my fingers around his girth and pumping his length up and down.

"Open up, Ana." He cupped the back of my head and brought me to the head of his cock.

Parting my lips, I engulfed the large, bulbous head, only taking him in a fraction of the way.

Sebastian tasted so different from Adrian—not better or worse, just different.

I licked the thick vein along the bottom of his erection as I came up and then enveloped more of him as I came down again. I swallowed, opening the back of my throat, trying not to gag.

"That's it, take him deep," Adrian commanded, giving

me the encouragement I hadn't known I'd needed. "Use that wicked tongue in the way I taught you. Make it so this will be a night he dreams of for the rest of his life."

As I worked Sebastian with my mouth and hand, Adrian gave me slow instructions and praise. After a little while, I no longer heard his crooning; all I could focus on was Sebastian's fingers flexing in my hair and the growing ache in my pussy.

Never before would I have imagined that I'd enjoy pleasuring a man other than Adrian. But there was something about Sebastian. I wouldn't lie to myself and say I wasn't attracted to him. And the arousal dripping down between my thighs would be a dead giveaway if I had thought to pretend otherwise.

I remembered the slight zing of interest when we'd met for the first time at UNLV and definitely when he'd arrived on the island. He was sexy and dark and mysterious. Plus, the German accent added to his appeal.

Sebastian's cock grew harder and to my surprise thicker.

"Fuck, I'm coming. Take. Every. Drop," he bit out as he clenched my hair and pulled me down with force, hitting the back of my throat and coming in thick, hard waves.

I swallowed and swallowed. God, how much cum was in one man? Some of it dripped from the sides of my lips.

When he loosened his hold on my head, I lifted my hand to wipe the cum from my face, but Sebastian stopped me, using his own fingers to collect his semen and push into my mouth.

"If this is the one time I get this, I don't want to waste any cum."

I sucked each of his offered digits, transfixed by this man who I couldn't see but knew was a walking god.

"Satisfied?" Adrian said, reminding me he was still in the room.

"No." Sebastian lifted me onto his lap, positioning my legs on either side of his thighs, his semi-erect cock sitting in the valley of my cleft. "But you've made her pussy off limits. Fuck, she's wet."

He drew me to him, kissing me, not caring he was tasting himself on me. He ground up against my clit as his tongue pushed past my lips.

What was it with these two men? They seemed to like the taste of their cum in my mouth. No wonder they were best friends.

"Not happening." Adrian growled, coming up behind me, gripping my hips and plucking me from Sebastian's grip as if I were a lightweight doll.

I grabbed hold of his arms, trying to keep my balance. Not that there was any chance I'd fall.

"She belongs to me. Don't ever forget it. Plus, the only child that will grow in her belly is mine."

I stiffened, hearing the absoluteness in Adrian's words.

I tilted toward him, wanting to ask if he truly was okay with a baby but kept it to myself.

Adrian brushed his lips against mine, then trailed his mouth over my jaw and whispered in my ear so only I could hear, "The only woman I've ever envisioned having children with is you."

Without asking permission, I tugged the blindfold from my eyes. I had to look at him to see if he was telling me the truth.

His emerald gaze burned with emotions. He was serious.

He loved me. It wasn't a question but more of my own realization.

He nodded, causing my vision to glaze with tears and throat to dry up.

Before I could say anything, he slid me down his body and said, "Undress me."

My hands shook but went immediately to the buttons of his shirt. Slowly, I unfastened them, holding his stare with each movement.

The intensity of what he'd shared gave me a sense of lightheadedness.

Pushing the cotton off his shoulders, I leaned up on tiptoes and kissed the pulse point below his ear.

"Ana." He growled and I noticed his breath growing shallow.

I smiled, feeling the power of how I affected him.

Had I ever seen a man as gorgeous as him? Sebastian was handsome and I was attracted to him, but no one made my heart race or ache the way this man did. He was mine. And it only took this fucked-up island to solidify the whole thing.

There was no going back to the way it was before. Hell, there was no going back to Solon. Would he come back home with me? That was a question we'd have to answer later.

I scratched my fingers down his chest and abdomen, feeling the bunch and release of his muscles. I loved touching him, stroking him. I loved his tattoos.

Opening his pants, I pushed them off his waist and let them pool at his feet. His cock was a hard, hot poker against my stomach. Precum wept from the tip, dampening my flesh.

My pussy contracted in response to his desire, adding to the arousal I'd felt from sucking Sebastian off.

As if on cue, Sebastian stepped behind me and bit the juncture between my neck and shoulder.

"Are you ready for us?" he asked.

How was I to answer? Until this situation, I'd never considered taking a man in my ass and pussy at the same time.

"As ready as I can be."

"Don't worry, baby. Weber will prepare you so you can take him."

Adrian threaded his fingers with mine and led me to the sofa. He sat, pulling me over him and then positioning my legs so I was straddling him. The press of his cock against my wet entrance felt right, and I so wanted him to push inside me.

"Soon, love. First, Weber's going to make you come." He shifted me up and back so my ass was spread.

That was when I heard the distinct sound of a bottle opening. Lube.

The next thing I felt was the gentle glide of Sebastian's finger sliding into my pussy and his lubed thumb pushing against my puckered rosette. At the same time, Adrian strummed my clit.

I whimpered, not in pain but from the sensation of so much stimuli at the same time. The second Sebastian breached my forbidden entrance, I arched up, impaling myself on his digits.

"Oh God. Why does this feel so good? More...I need to come."

Adrian took my clit and pinched it between his knuckles as Sebastian plunged in and out of me.

I came so hard, I saw stars. Adrian gripped the back of my neck, pulling my face to him. He devoured me as my pussy and ass clenched around Sebastian's fingers.

"She's ready. She's so wet, I could use the juices from her pussy instead of lube." He withdrew from my body and stood, stripping out of his clothes.

I glanced over my shoulder and took in the incredible body of the man behind me. Sebastian was ripped and covered in tattoos. He was leaner than Adrian but gorgeous nonetheless. Then there was that thick cock of his. He fisted it, pumping a few times as he covered it with the lube in his palm.

"Like what you see? Are you sure you prefer the Greek one over the German?"

"Don't make me kill you, Weber." Adrian moved me back up his body, growled "mine," and immediately thrust to the hilt inside me.

"Master," I cried out. My core quivered as he slid through the swollen tissues, my need always answering his.

He lifted and lowered me until I took over the movement, leveraging my palms on his shoulders and undulating my hips.

Another orgasm began to ripple, and just as I was about to go over, Sebastian said, "Lean forward, little dove. My turn to join the fun." Sebastian leveraged one knee on the sofa between Adrian's spread legs.

Adrian's hold on my hips tightened, and he held me down over his length. The heat of Sebastian behind me was like a brand on my back.

I was about to become an Ana sandwich.

Sebastian braced a hand on the back of the sofa and positioned his cock at my stretched hole. "I'll go slow."

I dropped my head to Adrian's shoulder, pressing my chest to his, feeling his cock throbbing in my pussy.

Adrian kissed my head. "Relax, it will make it easier."

Sebastian pushed past the tight ring of muscle, sliding in and out a fraction at a time, moving deeper and deeper with each shallow thrust.

"Goddamn, she is a fist," Sebastian gritted out.

By the time he was embedded all the way, my body was on overload, both literally and figuratively.

"Oh fuck." I clenched my teeth from the fullness of both men filling me.

It was too much. What were they thinking to believe I could handle two monster cocks?

Adrian cupped my face. "Breathe, baby."

I exhaled in a rush and immediately felt my muscles relax.

Both men pulsed in me, the only thing separating them a thin barrier of skin. They were furnaces around me, heating me from the inside and out. And on top of everything, God, did they smell good.

A quiver shot through me, and my pussy grew slicker.

"Master," I whimpered. "I need."

"I know." He drew my face to his, kissing me so deep that my core clenched and made both men moan.

"I'm going to have to move, Ana." Sebastian's voice was hoarse, and his fingers flexed on my hips as he slid out a faction and moved back in.

Adrian did the same, sliding through my pussy lips all the while still eating at my mouth.

I arched up and dug my fingers into his upper arms.

As one man pushed in, the other pulled out. They were an overload of hedonistic ecstasy.

Sebastian fisted my hair, jerking my head back, pulling me away from Adrian, and kissed me just as senseless. Adrian clasped onto my nipple, drawing it in with hard sucks to the rhythm of his thrusts.

I broke the kiss with Sebastian, and unable to take any more, my orgasm exploded out of me. My pussy and body convulsed and thrashed, riding wave after wave of pure, unadulterated pleasure. I was too lost in oblivion to realize that both men had come with me until their pistoning hips stopped their movements.

I collapsed on Adrian and muttered, "I think you two just killed me with orgasms."

CHAPTER FIFTEEN

Adrian

I walked out onto the deck, holding two cups of coffee. Sebastian watched the water, glancing at me and taking the mug I offered.

After a deep sip of the caffeinated brew, he asked, "Are you okay with what happened?"

I was still processing the night. After our collective orgasms, Sebastian and I cleaned up, turned off the surveillance giving Trevolo access to the bungalow, and then carried a very limp and wiped-out Ana to bed. We'd spent the night together with Ana sleeping between us.

When I'd woken, I expected to be upset but I wasn't. Sebastian was the only man I trusted with Ana and he hadn't let me down.

Last night had solidified Ana was mine. She needed me in a way I hadn't realized. Her pleasure came from not only what Sebastian had done to her but from the sheer fact I was there and she couldn't come unless I was the one to send her over.

She needed me as much as I needed her.

Once we finished this mission, I was going to marry her.

"You know as well as I do, I'm more than a bit possessive of Ana. But with that said, I'm okay with it."

Sebastian smirked, lifting the mug to his lips.

"Now I'm not saying that I want a repeat performance, but it wasn't the worst thing that could have happened."

"Admit it. You liked watching her do everything you said while another man worshiped her."

Not any man, only Sebastian. The fucker knew I viewed him as a brother.

"The point is irrelevant." I gazed out at the waves. "It's not happening again."

"You love her. Don't deny it."

"Never stopped."

"Does this mean you're getting out?"

I hadn't thought past rescuing Ana. But now that Sebastian had brought up the idea, I knew what I had to do.

"If I want a life with her, I don't have a choice. I waited five fucking years. This wasn't the way it was supposed to happen, but nothing with that woman goes according to plan."

"It's not going to be easy to get out."

"You think I don't know this?" I scrubbed a hand through my hair. "But I'll do what I have to so I'm free to go home."

"That means laying low. No glitzy wedding for the Lykaios brothers to splash all over the tabloids."

"If you knew anything about them, the last thing they'd want is a glitzy wedding. Plus, I have other things to worry about with them."

"Like?"

"Like the fact I'm going to spend the rest of my life with their baby sister. They are a bit overprotective, even if the world doesn't know they are related to Ana."

"It's not like you're some poor loser. Hell, man, your net worth could rival theirs."

"It's more the fact I was the boy they didn't want touching her from the beginning. They knew what I was into and didn't want it in Ana's life."

If the Lykaioses hadn't nearly killed me when they'd learned Ana and I had eloped, I would probably never have left her. They'd convinced me to let Ana pursue her dreams and let her go. I was a fucking idiot for listening. I should have taken the beating and told them to fuck themselves. If I had, she never would have gotten into this situation in the first place.

"In-laws, glad I don't have any," Sebastian mused, snapping me out of my regrets.

I snorted. "Fucker, you have the motherload when it comes to in-laws, or did you forget the wonderful arranged marriage your father is trying to hook you into going through with?"

Sebastian's father had recently informed him that to inherit leadership of the "family business," he'd have to marry the only daughter of the Becker family, a rival German organization that controlled territories adjacent to the Weber holdings. In other words, the two mobsters had negotiated a truce and the terms included an arranged marriage.

"It's not a done deal." He gripped the railing.

"You don't believe that any more than I do. You want to take the reins, then you know what you have to do."

"She's a pampered princess. Do you see someone like that enjoying the shit I do?"

"It's not like she has much choice in the matter. And you've done your research—she's not the diva you want her to be."

"It would be easier if she was."

I wanted to laugh. Sebastian was going to have his hands full with the rebellious princess who preferred her sniper rifles to designer gowns and purses. I was going to enjoy seeing how he handled marrying a hellion.

What the hell was I thinking? I was about to do the same damn thing.

"Now back to the subject of you moving on." Sebastian set his mug on the railing and turned to me. "I think I have a solution."

A naya

I woke feeling thoroughly used and satisfied. I never imagined that I'd enjoy being with two men, two very dominant men. Two men who knew exactly how to maneuver around each other.

It was obvious Adrian and Sebastian had shared women before, but for some reason I wasn't jealous anymore about the past. Maybe it was because of how possessive Adrian was of me or the fact he kept trying to convince me that we had a future once we left the island.

It was crazy to think the night he'd shared me with another man was the night he'd convinced me he truly loved me.

Adrian walked into the room with a mug.

"Is the feed off?" My body may want the coffee he held

but I had to ask. I'd been almost comatose when Adrian had carried me to bed.

He lifted a brow as if that was a stupid question. "Are you sore?"

I sat up, ready to get my caffeine fix.

Dear God, the man was a work of art, with tanned, ripped arms, chiseled abs, a "v" disappearing into low-hung lounge pants.

"Are you done ogling me?"

My cheeks heated. "Um, no, not really."

He shook his head but couldn't hide the smile that touched his lips.

He liked me looking at him as much as I liked it.

If we were in any other circumstance, I'd happily spend the day reacquainting myself with his delicious body.

"Are you sore?" he repeated.

I opened my mouth to say no but Adrian cut in.

"Don't lie."

I rolled my eyes and then sighed. "A little. But in a good way." I glanced behind him toward the living room. "Where's Sebastian?"

He moved closer, offering me the mug. "Gone."

I grabbed for it, drinking down the scalding liquid in a few gulps, letting the heat soothe my body and the caffeine begin its job of waking my brain cells.

"I will never understand how you can do that. Doesn't it burn your throat?"

I set the cup on the side table and smirked. "If I can handle two monster cocks, a little hot liquid isn't going to do anything."

"You'll only handle my cock from now on. That was a onetime thing. I will never share you again."

A sense of uneasiness washed over me. "Adrian, are you sure you're okay with what happened?"

"As I told Weber, yes I'm okay with it. I enjoyed it. However, let me repeat, it was a onetime thing."

"Then I guess you better satisfy me so I forget about the pleasures of two cocks."

Adrian glared at me for a second then something flashed in his eyes right before he pounced onto the mattress, grabbing my arms and pinning me to the bed.

"You want me to show you how well I can satisfy you with just one monster cock?" He rubbed his stubble against my neck, making me squirm.

I laughed. I hadn't seen this playful side of Adrian in over five years. I loved it.

"Are you laughing at me?" He loomed over me. "I'll give you something to laugh at."

He shifted my wrists to one of his hands and then dug the fingers of the other into the spot at my hip where only he knew I was ticklish.

"No." I bucked in between bouts of giggles. "Stop. No fair."

I tried to tug my arms free but to no avail. By the time he was finished torturing me, we were both out of breath and panting. My legs were wrapped around his waist and my bare chest pressed to his. Adrian released my wrists to thread his fingers into my hair.

Lowering his head, he sucked my lower lip into his mouth and then nipped it with his teeth.

Immediately my nipples tightened into hard buds and my cleft grew slick with desire. I gripped his arms, trying to bring him back for another kiss but he held still.

Adrian's emerald gaze burned into mine. "I love you, Ana. I never stopped."

My heart skipped a beat. I wanted to ask him why he'd left me if he loved me but I knew it wouldn't make a difference. Our breakup had given me the push I'd needed to succeed in a dangerous profession. He'd been the catalyst for proving my abilities.

"What does that mean for us?" I had to know.

"It means nothing outside of death is going to keep me from being with you again."

There was fierce determination on his face that showed me the truth of his words.

"Are you getting out?"

"That's the plan. But it may take time. I've been on this assignment for a long time. The higher-ups are going to have to find a plausible reason for why I all of a sudden disappeared."

I was in the same boat. Well maybe not as bad, since I hadn't lived as another person for years at a time. My debriefing would take about a month and then I'd go home.

Solon wasn't for me anymore. I'd accepted it. My place was with my family, with my annoying, overprotective brothers, my sister, my cousin, and my friends.

I was done running away.

He rubbed his thumb over my lips. "Are you willing to wait for me?"

That was a ridiculous question, but I realized he was truly worried.

"After all we've been through. You're asking me that?"

"Ana, answer the question."

"Of course, I'll wait."

His shoulders visibly relaxed, as if he was truly worried I wouldn't.

In this moment, he wasn't Julian or Adrian. He was my Ian. The boy I'd fallen so hard for.

For a split second, my heart ached to be back in Vegas in that tiny apartment he'd had in college.

"Ian?" I stared into his emerald eyes.

"Yeah?"

"Can we pretend for a few moments that we aren't in the middle of a mission where lives are on the line? That the only thing important is how we feel about each other?"

I needed to feel something that was just us. A connection without restraints. Without someone watching us and our most private moments.

He was quiet. Not saying anything.

Just when I expected him to tell me that it was impossible to expect more right now, he said, "Grab the slats of the headboard."

I threaded my fingers through the wood and held on.

My nipples immediately beaded and goosebumps prickled my skin.

The tenderness in his eyes turned feral. Whatever he had planned was something that would be a mix of pleasure and pain meant to drive me insane.

He rose, caging me with his arms and legs.

"I have one question for you and then you do everything I say. Gentle or hard?"

I held his hungry gaze. "Hard."

His lips quirked up at the sides. "Hard it is."

He reached over to the bedside table, opened a drawer, and pulled out a leather flogger.

My eyes grew wide. He'd had that in the bedside drawer this whole time?

Had he used it on the other women he'd bought in the harem auctions? A pang of jealousy shot through me.

He smacked the leather against his palm, pulling me from my thoughts. "I know what you're thinking. And to answer your unsaid questions, I have never used it on any other woman. It's sat in the drawer since Trevolo gave me the bungalow. The only woman's skin I've ever wanted to turn red from a flogger in my hand is yours."

I swallowed. "Oh."

"Yes, oh." He slapped his palm again. "Let's see how hard we can go."

Maybe I should have said gentle. The last time we'd played anything that was in the true realm of kink was when Adrian had taken me to one of the clubs in Vegas.

He'd chosen a place that wasn't owned by my brothers, a place where Adrian was a member. But that was a different time and a different Anaya.

"Ian."

"Ana."

He trailed the braided handle over my pubic bone, across my stomach, and up my neck.

"The straps are suede, not the harder leather we used long ago. You aren't ready for that."

Was I even ready for this? From my memory, suede stung pretty bad. The only benefit was that the marks disappeared faster.

"Don't let go or I won't let you come."

My pulse pounded into my ears and my fingers clenched the slats.

"Relax, baby." He guided the multitude of soft leather straps over my face and down my body, circling my breasts, teasing my navel, and grazing my cleft.

He stroked all over my body, hypnotizing me with his movements. Slowly I began to relax into the bed.

Smack.

"Oh fuck." I arched up as the sting of the leather straps shot over my abdomen.

I should have known the second I relaxed he'd start.

Dammit, Ana, just because it's been five years doesn't mean you forget the way of things.

Smack. Smack.

The next ones hit my outer thighs.

"Ian." I moaned and thrashed, unable to shift my legs because of Adrian's weight on them.

How the hell had I forgotten it hurt so damn much?

Smack. Smack. Smack.

Tears streamed down my face as I bit my lips.

Adrian shifted off my legs and leaned over my face, cupping it. "Breathe, baby, let the endorphins take over."

I whimpered in response.

Adrian licked my tears. "You're so beautiful, so perfect for me. Now do as I say."

I inhaled and then exhaled; the pain of the leather began to morph into a warm, dull ache. My nipples responded and my core clenched.

"You ready for more?"

I nodded without a second thought.

Smack. Smack. Smack.

This time the sting was there but the pleasure came

right along with it. His strikes landed all over my body but now I arched into the graze of the suede.

My pussy wept and clenched as my mind clouded.

"I need to come. I need to come. Ian, please let me come."

He dropped the flogger to the side and slipped a finger deep inside my pussy, curving in just enough to hit the bundle of sensitive tissue that encompassed my G-spot.

I convulsed around him, milking his fingers as my body finally got the reward of release.

He pulled out, bringing his fingers to my lips. "Suck."

I followed his directions, letting the taste of my essence add to the high of release.

"Now it's my turn. You know the rules, Ana. Don't let go."

Pushing down his pants, his beautiful thick, hard cock sprang free. Adrian spread my legs, positioned his cock, and slammed in.

"This is going to be hard, just the way you asked for it." He pulled out and shot in.

"Oh God," I gasped.

He fucked me like a madman. The only thing keeping me from smacking my head against the headboard was my hold on the slats.

"I need you so fucking much, Ana," he said between breaths.

"I need you too." I wanted so desperately to hold him, dig my nails into his ass.

"Fuck, I can't hold back." He squeezed his eyes shut and roared, "Mine. My woman. Mine."

He came and came, pumping so hard that it pushed me into another orgasm.

I cried out, arching against him and clamping down on his still-thrusting cock. All of a sudden, he pulled out, slid down my body, and fastened his mouth to my pussy.

He ate at me, not caring that his cum was coating my body.

"Oh God, Ian." I dropped a hand into his hair, causing him to growl and bite my inner thigh.

"Ow," I whimpered, but my arousal and need didn't ebb. In fact, they were heightened by the pain.

"Hand. Move it back."

I gripped the headboard again. His tongue flicked and thrust until he'd wrung another orgasm out of me. Then he crawled up my body and drove his cock into my contracting core.

The man was a fucking machine.

He grabbed my throat, squeezing with each thrust.

"One more time."

Was he out of his mind? He could go all night, but my body was all done with orgasms. My pussy was too swollen, too sensitive

"No. Please. It's too much. I can't."

A moan escaped my lips and a tremor shot through my core, my body betraying my words.

Adrian pressed harder against my windpipe. "I say when you come, not you. Who owns this body, Ana? Who owns you?"

He pistoned hard and fast as he loomed over me. Sweat dripped from his temples, and the dark, feral lust I saw had my core quivering.

"You do."

Thrust. Thrust. Thrust.

"If I say I want one more, what do you say?"

"Yes, Ian."

Thrust. Thrust. Thrust.

"Now come."

He held my throat as he pummeled my pussy, and with one hard roll of his hips, I exploded again.

"Ian," I cried out, my vision a complete blur except for this man above me.

I was still coming when he pulled out, gripped his cock in his hands, and pumped his cum all over my stomach and pussy.

"Fucking beautiful," he panted out and pressed his body to mine a second before he kissed me.

CHAPTER SIXTEEN

Adrian

"You can let go now," I said to Ana as I rolled to the side, pulling my weight off her body. "We need to shower. We're covered in cum."

I couldn't figure out what had come over me. It was this insane urge to mark Ana. To have my cum brand her as mine. Maybe it was the fact we were stealing this time for ourselves in the middle of a fucked-up situation and I wasn't sure when I'd be able to touch her like that again.

"Back to reality and our jobs," she said, releasing her hold on the slats, and then turning to me. "We need to end this sooner rather than later."

"That's the plan." I stared into her amber depths. "We

can't do this again until we're back home. We can't afford to let our guard down."

"I know." Her tone has a tinge of remorse and she looked away, closing her eyes.

"What's wrong?"

"I didn't expect to feel so guilty for taking time for a little bit of comfort."

She wasn't the only one having those emotions. There were people arriving on this island that wouldn't have a sliver of a chance at comfort or happiness, unless we helped them.

I took her hand in mine.

"Ana. We—"

A hard knock echoed into the bedroom and both Ana and I stiffened.

What the fuck? My monitoring system should have alerted me of anyone approaching. That's when I realized my watch was on the side table.

Reaching over to grab it, I pushed a button and an image appeared on the small screen of Trevolo with some of his henchmen waiting outside.

"Fuck. Trevolo's here." I got out of the bed. "Ana, go shower. And no matter what you hear, do not come out."

She looked like she was about to argue, but then said, "Okay," and slipped from the bed.

I shrugged on my pants and grabbed a T-shirt I'd

thrown on a table, not caring the remnants of fucking Ana were stuck to my body.

I unlocked and pushed open my front door. "Want to tell me what's so important that you came personally to my bungalow to chat?"

Trevolo seemed unfazed by my words. "Something has come to my attention and I thought it best to speak of this in person."

Well, that sounded ominous.

I widened the door to let Trevolo in but blocked it when his guards tried to enter. "You know the rules," I said to the one in front. "You can stay out here as usual or fuck off. I don't care."

Before the guard could protest, Trevolo spoke. "Dante, wait outside. Mr. Bonaparte isn't going to hurt me, especially since he spends a great deal of time ensuring my safety with his gadgets."

I slammed the door closed and moved into the living area where Trevolo made himself at home in an armchair. He eyed the sofa.

"Your scene last night was very entertaining."

My temper prickled knowing Trevolo and countless others had to have watched, probably live.

"It was." I moved to sit on the couch where Sebastian and I attended Ana last night. "Did you learn anything?"

I should have kept my tone calm and left out the latter part of my statement, but I couldn't help it.

"It would have been better if you respected my authority and left the audio on. The sound of a woman's cries of pleasure and pain are music to my ears."

Saying "more pain than pleasure" was on the tip of my tongue but I managed to keep it in.

Something unpleasant was about to happen and I had to keep it together.

"Where is your bride?" He glanced at the closed bedroom door.

"Recovering."

He scoffed. "From last night? Hardly. She took a beating and stood up to punch my guards. And let's not forget her handling of Mica Chance. The woman would have to be bound and flogged to make it so she needed to recover."

I gave a condescending smirk. "As a matter of fact, a flogger was involved in our morning activities."

A flash of surprise crossed Trevolo's face, then was replaced by smug satisfaction. "I'm glad Aphrodite's pussy hasn't made you soft. I worried it had come to that."

"Never mistake indulging a new toy as going soft. I am the same man I was when we met. I'm only taking care of my twenty-million-dollar toy."

"That is the reason I'm here."

I lifted a brow. "The money cleared before I took possession of my bride. Is there a problem?"

"Your money arrived as you said. It is another matter. Weber came to me with a proposition this morning."

"I'm listening."

"He offered me double what you paid to acquire your bride."

What the fuck was Sebastian doing? This was not part of our plan.

"Since my money cleared, this is a moot point."

"Ah, but it's not. I'm a businessman, and Weber is willing to pay a nice fee to you for your inconvenience. This is a win/win for both of us."

Like hell it was a win/win. I had to keep my emotions in check, or I'd let the fucker bait me into showing him what Ana meant to me.

Then it hit me, the only reason Sebastian would change the plan was because our time had run out. A text on the sat phone would have been a better warning than orchestrating this shit. Who was I kidding? If plans changed, it had come from the higher-ups.

I really hoped Ana wouldn't neuter me when this was over.

"How much for my inconvenience?" I rose and walked to the bar in the corner of the room. "Want some?"

Trevolo eyed the Firewater Black Reserve bottle. "Of course. You're the only one I know who stocks this brand of whiskey as if it were available in a convenience store. Isn't this bottling almost impossible to find?"

The reason I had unfettered access to Firewater, a whiskey that had taken the spirit world by storm, was because the company belonged to my sister. I always packed a bottle or two when I traveled, and it came in handy as a tool to get people playing on my side. Offer some fucker a thousand-dollar-an-ounce award-winning whiskey as a gesture of good faith and they'd sell their firstborn for more.

"Almost impossible. I have connections." I offered Trevolo the glass with the amber liquid. "What is my inconvenience fee?"

"Half of what you paid me. And of course, I will return your payment and offer you a seat at the auction."

"What kind of auction?"

"The special kind." He gave me a calculated smile. "The kind your precious dove should have been part of."

As if I believed the bastard was going to go through with having me at his special auction. Having me anywhere near anything to do with selling children would be a grave error on his part.

The fucker planned to double-cross me and thought I was stupid enough not to see through his bullshit.

"And when will this event take place?"

"Tonight."

Fuck, that meant the shipment of women and children had arrived either yesterday or earlier today.

God. Sebastian and my preoccupation with Ana had

been the perfect opportunity for Trevolo to unload the women and children.

"Did you offer this option to Weber?"

"Yes, but I didn't push. His way puts more money in both of our pockets. What say you?"

I pondered and then said, "I will have to consider it and get back to you."

"You do that." His lips quirked up as if he knew I was going to accept.

"What if I said I'm not finished with her?"

"Fuck her and beat her a few more times. Weber doesn't care what you do to her, as long as she is his when he leaves the island tonight."

"What about the other guests? Won't you lose too much goodwill when you cut their vacations short?"

A gleam entered his eyes. "Mr. Finn was the only one I knew would have no interest in the special auction. He left this morning to take care of a family emergency. The rest are invited guests as you are."

Well, fuck. Everyone outside of Finn knew what Trevolo was setting up—the two-week pleasure vacation was only a front until the human cargo arrived. It wouldn't surprise me if Trevolo set up Finn's family troubles to get him off the island faster.

This also meant Sebastian's arrival wasn't only to keep Ana's team from invading the island to rescue her. Having him on the island meant there was another person around to collect evidence.

"What say you to my offer?"

"As I said. I'll consider it."

Irritation flashed across his face. "This isn't optional, Bonaparte. I'm sure your father would agree it isn't wise to throw away a profitable arrangement for some used pussy." Trevolo set his tumbler on the coffee table and moved to the door.

"Dante will be here in a few hours to escort your bride to her new master. Fuck her to your heart's content until then."

Trevolo left, shutting the door behind him. I waited a few minutes before I let the rage take over and hurled my glass across the room, shattering it against the wall near the front door.

Ana stepped into the room. From the worry etched on her face, she'd listened to every word of my conversation with Trevolo.

"Are you going to hand me over to Sebastian?"

"I let another man fuck you in front of Trevolo and God knows who else to get you off the island. What do you think?"

"Will they expect me to have sex with Sebastian again?"

"Who knows? Probably. I don't know."

The thought of it was like a knife in the heart. But if it meant Ana was safe...

Her eyes widened. "Not happening. That was a onetime thing."

"You said you enjoyed it."

She glared at me and stalked in my direction. "I did but that doesn't mean it's something I want to experience again and especially not with others as if they were watching live-action porn."

"Ana. The women and children are here. You heard Trevolo. He's auctioning them tonight." I pulled her to me, wrapping her in my arms. "This is what we've been working for. I'm going to hand you over to Sebastian."

A naya

"The hell you are. We are a team. At this moment, I'm not your woman. I'm your Solon partner." I couldn't believe what I was hearing. He really thought I was going to sit back and let him do all the dirty work.

"It's the only way to get you off this island without risking your life. I won't be able to focus or relay the right information if I'm worried about you."

"If Trevolo's goons come anywhere near me, I swear I will break every one of their noses."

"They aren't going to come near you. I'm giving you to Sebastian in the next hour."

"You've got to be out of your mind. I'm not going anywhere."

"Ana, listen to me. I hand you over early, then Sebastian can leave with you. No matter what he says to Trevolo, his yacht is within thirty minutes of here."

"And what are you going to be doing in the meantime?"

"I'm going to finish my assignment and free those women and children who have been through God knows what."

"What about Ele?"

"She isn't part of my mission, but I planned to get Ele back to her family too."

"Her sister sold her. That's not family."

"Her parents mourn her every day. With Trevolo here I can have his bitch wife handled."

It sounded so easy, so feasible, but it wasn't something I believed would go off without a hitch.

"And what am I supposed to do sitting on Sebastian's yacht? I'm not really a sit-back-and-let-the-menfolk-save-the-day kind of girl." I cocked a hand on my hip.

His lips quirked up. "As if I didn't know this."

"I'm serious, Ian."

"Figure out the best way to tell your brothers you're marrying me."

I wasn't sure what to say to that. He'd mentioned being together during passion but marriage? Again?

"Nothing to say about that?" He slipped an arm around my waist and drew me to him. "I love you, baby. Let me save the day this one time. You can be your badass Selene self another day."

There wouldn't be another day. I was leaving Solon. I was ready to be home, with my family, with Adrian. I'd barely spent any time with anyone in Vegas for so long that I missed so many things, especially the births of my nephews. And now Henna was expecting a girl. The only one out of all the Lykaios kids. I wanted to be there.

"Ian, nothing is as easy as you are saying it'll be. What if something goes wrong? At least give me a gun or something."

"And where do you plan to hide it in your see-through clothes?"

I glanced down and sighed. "Point taken."

"Now go get ready. We are going to make a surprise visit to the main house. And if anything goes wrong, take the path leading left at the bottom of the terrace stairs. There's a small cave along the cliff. Wait there for me." He pulled out a satellite phone, typed something, and then dropped it to the ground, crushing it.

"What did you just do?"

"Called my ride. But first we need to get you on yours."

We made our way to the main house to hear loud shouts and the sobs of a woman.

Adrian pressed a finger to his lips and then pushed me behind him.

"You know the punishment for disobeying me. Do you want me to give you to the men?" Trevolo's rage was evident, and I feared for whomever he was yelling at.

"Your threats don't scare me anymore. You've already taken everything from me. My child, my life," Ele screamed back at him. "Do what you have to."

Child?

I tugged on Adrian's sleeve. He shook his head.

"What has come over you? Since when does it bother you to get the information I want?"

"Since you took our child from me and gave him to your bitch wife. Since you whored me out to your highest-paying clients."

Holy fuck. The baby Catarina Trevolo had given birth to wasn't hers. Hell, she'd never been pregnant. Her weight gain had been a show, and the fact she was so pissed off that her gowns didn't fit was because it wasn't baby weight she had to lose.

Dear God, that sweet little boy was Ele's, and they'd stolen him from her.

"You make it sound like I pass you around from man to man. It was two times. I had no choice—they asked for you."

"And now you are handing me out again?"

"Bonaparte is losing the prize he is taken with. I have to do something to keep the bastard happy."

"But why me?"

"Because you are the most valuable jewel on the island to me. He knows it as does everyone else. If he accepts you, then there is no need for him to attend the auction and risk the trouble he could give me about the items on sale."

"Give them someone else. Your favorite, perhaps, but not me. There are countless women willing to spread their legs for him."

"There is no other choice. He likes you. I've seen him look at you. Do you think I want the bastard touching what's mine?"

Adrian glanced at me, as if trying to convey something. Then it hit me. He was worried about what Trevolo said.

I shook my head at him—I knew he had no feelings about Ele outside of getting her out of her situation.

"I'm not yours. You took me from my family, raped me, and then stole my child. I will always hate you."

The hard echo of a slap reverberated from the terrace.

"Ungrateful bitch."

That was when Adrian grabbed my hand and pulled me up the steps.

"Are we disturbing anything?" Adrian drawled, forcibly jerking me forward and causing me to fall to the ground where Ele sat covering her cheek with her hands.

I gasped and glared at him.

"Not at all." Trevolo examined me with a smirk. "Trouble in paradise?"

"Call Weber. I see no point in wasting time. She's ready to go."

"What caused the change of mind?"

"There is no point in training a slave for another man, no matter how sweet the cunt."

"Ele, get up and call Weber. Once he leaves, the island will be clear. We will start our auction."

Ele stared at me. It was easy to see her rage and hate for the man who'd taken so much from her.

"Did you hear me?" Trevolo towered over Ele.

Ele nodded, pushing herself to standing. Then, after she caught her breath, she turned and left.

I remained on the ground, looking between the two men who watched my every reaction.

"Come sit, Anastasia." Trevolo pulled out a chair.

I rose and sat on the chair.

"Whatever training you put her through has worked. I expected her to stand up and try to either punch or kick me."

I'll oblige you, fucker, if you'd like.

"Ana knows that there are consequences for bad behavior and rewards when she listens."

"I've been thinking." Trevolo ran a finger along my neck, making my skin crawl. "How would you feel if I gave you something more valuable than a chance to bid in the auction?"

Adrian folded his hands and leaned against the railing. "I'm listening. What is it you are offering?"

"Elenora."

"Let me get this straight. You are offering me your prized house mistress?"

"Yes."

"To keep?"

Trevolo stopped his strokes on my skin and I was grateful, but his hands moved to the back of my chair, gripping it tight and all but making it crack. "Yes."

This was so bizarre. No, it was fucked up on a whole crazy level. Trevolo had feelings for Ele. I doubted it was more than viewing her as property, but the thought of giving her to anyone didn't sit well with him.

"At what cost do I get Elenora?"

"For your bride and your departure from my home." He paused. "Immediately."

"And the monetary compensation we agreed to previously?"

"It stands."

"Then there is nothing left to say but done."

No one said anything for a few minutes, but I could feel Trevolo's agitation.

If Adrian left with Ele, then how was he going to get the women and children out? There had to be a plan B he hadn't told me about.

That thought pissed me off, but I had to stay in character. He was so going to get a piece of my mind when we were alone again.

Footsteps echoed from inside the house, and the second Sebastian and Ele came into view, Trevolo said, "She's yours. Take her and leave."

"What?" Ele looked between Trevolo and Adrian.

"Your master has given you to me," Adrian said, stepping in her direction.

Her eyes clouded with tears. Something told me they weren't tears of sadness.

Sebastian walked toward me, holding my gaze. "Does this mean you are relinquishing claims on this creature?"

"Yes. Enjoy her."

"Oh, I will. There is no doubt." Sebastian's tone was amused. "I may invite you as a third in the future if you aren't too busy with Elenora."

"Now, gentlemen. I believe it is time for both of you to leave." Trevolo's voice was calm but the clenching of his fingers on the back of the chair told me he was anything but.

Before anyone could move, a group of helicopters approached at a fast speed.

"What the fuck is that?" Adrian demanded of Trevolo.

"You tell me. You're the security expert."

"Get down," Sebastian yelled, just as a shot echoed in the air.

Grabbing Ele's arm, I pulled her under a set of tables. "Stay down, Ele."

"Ana, go now," I heard Adrian shout. "The copters are circling back around. I don't want you to get caught in the crossfire when Trevolo's security comes out."

"Who are they?" I asked Sebastian who was crouched behind another table.

He didn't answer, only said, "Get to safety, now. Your people will kill me if anything happened to you."

I tried to identify the aircraft, having no luck until the all-black helicopters turned, revealing a small scorpion on their tails.

It was Solon.

"Dammit, Ana, stop stalling and go," Adrian yelled.

I scanned the area for him but couldn't see where he was.

Ele and I rushed out from under the table and stopped as we saw Trevolo covered in blood from a bullet wound to the head and lying on the ground with his eyes open.

He'd been the target.

Ele rushed to him, kicking him and spitting on his face. "I hate you. I hate you. I hate you."

I dragged her away, taking the path Adrian had said led to the cave.

"Stay close."

"Who are you, really?"

"Just someone like you who got caught by the scum of the earth."

We made it to the beach in record time, using the foliage as cover. A wave of gunfire echoed from the main house, followed by shouts.

"Let's go, Ele."

In the distance I saw a yacht. That had to be Sebastian's. Then I noticed two speedboats approach the beach.

"That's our ride, Ele. We'll hide in the cave until we see Ian and Sebastian."

Ele tilted her head. "You call them by their first names?" Then her eyes grew wide. "You knew them before here."

"It's complicated. We will fill you in, once we get to safety."

That was when I noticed Sebastian and Adrian heading toward the speedboats. I heard Adrian calling me to come toward him. Just as Adrian looked in my direction, Sebastian pulled out a gun and shot him in the chest.

Adrian jerked back, collapsing on the sand.

CHAPTER SEVENTEEN

Anaya

"Noooo," I screamed.

This couldn't be happening. Not after all we'd come through.

I'd finally gotten him back.

Why? Sebastian was his friend. Why would he do this? None of this made sense.

Tears filled my eyes as I fell to the ground.

I watched in horror as uniformed men picked Adrian up and carried him to the rowboat, all but throwing his limp body in.

I had to get to him. I couldn't let them throw him away like he was nothing.

"Ana." Ele tugged at me. "We have to get to safety. We

have to find a place to hide."

I pushed down the pain of my heart shattering and nodded. "The cave. Ian said we'd be safe in the cave."

"I know where it is. Follow me. It's this way."

We ran into the tropical forest, Ele leading the way.

Just as we reached a clearing, two men jumped out, grabbing us.

"Let me go, you bastard." I fought the hold on me, punching the man in the face.

"Fuck."

His grip broke as he fell to the sand, bleeding.

That was when I heard Ele struggling. She wasn't trained—I had to help her.

A knife would have really come in handy right now.

I ran toward Ele, jumping on the attacker's back. He slammed me into a tree, but I held on to his neck. With my weight keeping him off balance, he dropped Ele, giving me enough time to choke him until he passed out.

"Hurry," Ele called.

We rushed down a narrow path but stopped dead in our tracks when Sebastian stepped in front of us.

"Not so fast, little dove." He sounded nothing like the man I'd known for years.

"You bastard. How could you? You..." I couldn't get the words out.

He grabbed me by the hair and pulled me toward him.

"What did I do? I got rid of a troublesome asshole who thought he ruled the nest."

"He trusted you. He let you…" I trailed off, feeling disgusted by the night we'd had together.

"He let me taste his prize because he had no choice. I bought you. Now you're permanently mine."

"Like hell I am." I elbowed him in the stomach, but he didn't even flinch.

His grip only got tighter. "You think that's supposed to hurt. I grew up at the knee of Liam Weber. Pain is a meal he served regularly."

One of the men who attacked Ele and me reached us, wheezing and out of breath.

"Could have told me she packed a punch. Jace is knocked out cold."

"What would be the fun in that?" Sebastian smirked and pulled out a syringe.

I began to thrash and then clamped my nails onto his arm. Then my training kicked in and I swept my leg behind me, hitting the back of Sebastian's knee.

"Motherfucker."

We both toppled to the ground.

"Dammit, Ana."

All of a sudden, my mind grew heavy and I couldn't lift my head.

The last thing I heard as I lost consciousness was, "You

never make anything easy, do you? No wonder he loves you so much."

I woke to the feeling of extreme nausea. My head hurt and my body ached.

Where was I?

That was when it came to me.

Adrian.

Oh God. Oh God. Oh God.

I wrapped my arms around my waist, keeping my eyes closed and letting tears soak my face.

How was I going to go back home and tell Penny and my family what had happened? That was if I made it out of this alive.

Adrian had worried about me coming home in a body bag and now it was me who had to live with the very real scenario.

My body jumped and I realized I was on some type of boat. Opening my eyes, I looked around.

What the fuck.

I was on a king-sized bed in some kind of high-end cabin. Everything was polished and new. It looked so much like the yacht Henna owned. This had to be the owner's suite.

I glanced down at my clothes and I was no longer in

the godawful sheer gown. Instead, I wore soft cotton lavender pajamas.

Anger rose like a raging fire. If for one second Sebastian thought I'd let him replace Adrian, he had another think coming.

I'd spent too many days pretending to be something I wasn't. I'd fight until I died.

I jumped out of the bed, stumbling as a wave of dizziness hit me.

Fucking drug.

After a few breaths, I had myself under control.

I moved to the attached bathroom. After using the facilities, I searched the cabinets for anything I could use as a weapon.

"Jackpot."

In a drawer was a straight razor. I was well versed in the use of this baby.

I tucked it into the back of my pants.

I moved back into the cabin, going toward the door. Pressing my ear to the steel, I listened for any sound.

It was quiet.

I stepped into the hallway, worked my way up a set of stairs.

What time was it? There was barely anyone about.

Pushing that thought back, I made my way to the main salon of the ship.

The sound of conversation carried toward me with the breeze of the ocean.

It was Sebastian.

I pulled the blade from my pants.

Even if I died, I was going to maim the motherfucker.

I approached a corner and pressed myself against a wall in the shadows when a guard passed.

"She should be awake soon," Sebastian said. "Damn woman nearly dislocated my knee."

"Well, you're the one who came at her with a syringe. What the hell did you expect?" said Jacob Castro.

What the hell was he doing here?

Jacob was the head of Solon operations in Southern Europe. I'd dealt with him on and off for years. He'd retired from active assignments and only came into the field for extractions.

"Her reaction was mild compared to what I'd do to you, Weber," Briana Amici said with a hint of amusement in her words. "I'd have stabbed that needle in your dick."

Was this all a setup?

Hope began to bloom deep in my chest.

"That is not the visual I need at the moment, Amici."

"What? I'm just telling you the truth. You should be used to me by now. Isn't this the sixth joint project we've worked on?"

"Seventh." Sebastian groaned again. "I'm going to have to ice my leg for the next few weeks to get back to normal."

"Stop bitching. We had to get an honest reaction or there was no way lover boy here was going to get out. The timing for the copters could have been better, but it worked. They got Trevolo."

What the hell? Adrian. He was alive.

The pain in my chest eased for the first time since I saw him go down.

I moved closer.

"Well, it's done. Now it's time to clean up the mess that is Catarina Island," Jacob said. "Amici will take charge of the women and children and we'll let you CIA boys handle the garbage tucked away in Trevolo's dungeon. Weber will handle Elenora."

"You guys go right ahead and take over. I'm fucking tired. Did you have to shoot me three times? Damn vest only protects you so much. I'm going to have bruises for a month."

I dropped the blade, letting it bang on the floor.

Everyone in the room froze as they saw me.

"Ana." Adrian stared at me with surprise.

My hands shook.

Then, all of a sudden, my relief was replaced by anger.

I walked up to him, ignoring everyone else I planned to deal with in a few moments.

Wariness shadowed his gaze, and just as Adrian reached out to touch me and opened his mouth to say something, I punched him as hard as I could in the gut.

CHAPTER EIGHTEEN

Adrian

"How could you?" she screamed at me.

I tried to answer but all I could do was attempt to breathe through the pain.

"Fucking hell, woman, you and your sneaky moves," Sebastian said and stayed in his spot near the window.

He should have been the first person to sense Ana or anyone approach. He was definitely getting rusty.

I straightened, taking a step toward her, but that was when Jacob made the mistake of grabbing Ana's arms to keep her from punching me again.

She twisted so fast that he ended up on the ground.

"Goddammit. You're not supposed to use the very moves I taught you on me."

She ignored Jacob and trained her pissed-off-to-holy-hell eyes on me.

God, she was magnificent. And my cock thought so too as it jumped.

"Ana. Baby."

She stalked to me and jabbed a finger in my bruised chest.

"How could you?" Tears clouded her amber depths. "I thought you were dead. I thought...I thought... Damn you. Why couldn't you have told me?"

"Bella, you know how this works. You've been in the game long enough," Briana said with a smirk as she buffed her manicured nails against her too-fucking-expensive-for-fieldwork shirt.

"I will get to you later," Ana bit out as she held my gaze. "Am I such an amateur that you couldn't have filled me in?"

I slid my arms around her waist and pulled her to me, ignoring the pain from the bullet impacts. The fact she wrapped her arms around me was one positive in this whole fucked-up situation that I could live with.

She inhaled, taking in my scent, and then her body shook.

"We had to. Too many eyes were on us and we had to make it look as real as possible."

She lifted a hand to her face. "Bullshit. I knew how to act. I've done it for the last week and a half."

I cupped the back of her head and couldn't help but grin down at her. "Maybe with most people around you but not with me. And not with Trevolo. He knew how you felt about me. You're in love with me."

She shoved me but I held her tight.

"Bella, admit it," Briana said in her thick Italian accent. "We all know the truth. He's the reason you ran away to join the Solon circus."

Ana glared at her. "And you joined because you ran away from an arranged marriage to a man you always wanted to marry anyway."

"Yes, but your man isn't a mobster."

"Neither is yours."

"It's all a matter of perspective. Financing them is just as bad." Briana folded her arms across her chest and met Ana's annoyed glare with her own.

I knew it was time for us to be alone or this whole thing was about to get derailed.

"Gentlemen and lady. Would you mind leaving us?"

"Oh, come on. I was beginning to enjoy this." Sebastian laughed as he stood.

For a man who spent most of his day scowling, he was a downright comedian when the world wasn't watching.

The end of this assignment meant the end of our association. The end of our ten-year friendship. It was inevitable. He could never leave the world, and Ana was my escape.

As sad as losing Sebastian as a partner and friend was, it also meant I had Ana.

"Get out," I ordered.

"Make it fast or I may have to get nosy," Briana cooed, walking out, but she stopped midway and added, "Remember, debriefing waits for no one. Especially when it is the final one."

What the fuck did that mean? That woman was something else. Always talking in crazy riddles. Then it hit me. They knew Ana was leaving Solon.

How the hell did they know? She'd only decided on the island.

Jacob followed, pointing to his watch.

"If you assholes would get out of here, I could talk to my woman."

"He's only reminding you that groveling is time sensitive." Sebastian walked up to Ana, touching her cheek. "If you ever decide to get adventurous again, count me in as the third."

I growled. "Keep dreaming, asshole. It was a onetime thing."

"Worth a try." Sebastian walked out of the lounge whistling to himself.

Ana pulled away from me and moved to a bench seat near the window. I knew keeping her out of the loop was going to have repercussions. I just couldn't risk anything going wrong, especially with Sebastian putting a monkey wrench in the original plan with his bid to buy Ana out from under me.

"Can you forgive me, baby?"

Her gorgeous golden amber eyes burned into mine. "Yes. Don't scare me like that again."

"What happens now?" I asked.

"You tell me."

Trust her to throw it back at me.

"Marriage, babies, a normal life." Until I said the words aloud, I hadn't realized how much I wanted those things with Ana.

She visibly swallowed and her lip trembled, but she kept quiet.

We stared at each other, then when I couldn't stand it anymore, she said, "Okay."

"No more Solon."

"No more CIA."

"No more mob prince."

"No more fashion assistant, mob princess, or Selene the Lycan slayer." Her face softened into a brilliant smile, and my heart clenched. She took a step toward me. "Deal."

"I love you, Ana." I moved in her direction.

"I..." Ana trailed off as the sounds of helicopters echoed all around us. "Dammit. I thought I had more time."

"What the fuck is going on?"

Ana lifted her hands to stay me. "Ian, no matter what, don't fight them."

Next thing, a group of people dressed in black from head to toe filed in, one grabbing Ana and the others moving in my direction.

She struggled. "Let go. Could you have given me a few more minutes?"

I rushed toward her but was knocked down by a woman at least five inches shorter than Ana who was midway between me and where Ana was being held. "Calm down. We aren't going to hurt her."

Another man pointed a gun in my face. "Stand down. If we hurt you, she'll kick our ass. But I'll do it, if you don't listen."

"As if." I grabbed the barrel to knock it out of the fucker's hands, but another two men pinned my shoulders.

"You know procedure, Anthony. Protocol requires immediate evac. No stalling. No wasting time. Tell him to calm the fuck down," the pint-sized woman said again, coming over to me and glaring down at me with what looked almost like amusement.

I had the distinct feeling I knew her.

"Ian. I'm sorry. I have to go." I watched in disbelief as the group all but dragged Ana toward the door. "I promise, I'm okay. It's the way they say goodbye. I love you."

She disappeared from view.

I struggled against the linebackers holding me down. "Where the fuck are you taking her?"

"Hold still, asshole. You should know how this works. Get a grip."

Debriefings at the CIA never involved an extraction scenario. Fucking Solon. They never did anything like normal people. Always so damn dramatic.

"Fuck you," I yelled at the shithead pressing his foot to my windpipe.

"You CIA snobs believe you have all the control. It's only because we let you have it. You're lucky we like your pal Weber, otherwise we wouldn't give a shit if your operation was compromised. She's ours too. Let us say goodbye."

Like hell she was theirs.

"Put him in the chair."

Immediately, I was hauled up and thrown in a chair, guns trained at my head.

The pint-sized lady stalked toward me, pulling off the ski mask that covered her face.

Holy fuck. I couldn't believe what I was seeing.

"Adrian Kipos. It's good to finally meet the man who helped recruit one of the best agents I've ever worked with by breaking her heart." I just stared at the hand she offered. "I believe you know me as the first lady."

CHAPTER NINETEEN

Anaya

I inhaled the warm, dry air of the desert as I watched the lights on the Las Vegas Strip from the open-air deck of my penthouse apartment at the top of the Ida Resort and Casinos.

It had been two months since I left Adrian on the yacht and three weeks since I returned to Vegas. My family had given me space, surprisingly accepting that I'd quit my job because I was on the verge of burnout.

For years they'd tried to get me to come home and take over Henna's business empire, without any headway. The fact I'd just up and made the decision had to have nagged at them. It surprised me they hadn't ambushed me by now, demanding answers.

I knew I had to do a better job of behaving like I was happy with my decision. I hadn't expected how hard it was going to be to live as a normal person and not a spy. Even going back to my natural hair color and clothing style hadn't made it easier. I felt like an imposter in my real-life persona.

Was I going to be able to do this?

You don't have a choice, Anaya. You can't go back. This is a done deal.

The years on the job had left a toll on me, both mentally and physically. No matter the cost, I knew I'd made a difference. Especially with this last assignment. I'd played a pawn to get the job done and, in the end, Ele and so many others were safe.

I sighed, thinking of Ele. I wanted so badly to know where she was and how she was doing but I knew there was no possibility of contact for either of us. Leaving Solon meant stepping away from everything.

Well, with the exception of Briana. She was kind of a permanent fixture in my real life. But she knew the job better than I did and would never break protocol.

Picking up a glass of sparkling water from a nearby table, I took a sip and watched a helicopter land on a neighboring building.

I really had a kickass view from up here. The penthouse used to belong to my brother Hagen, but he'd moved to a house in the burbs with my cousin Penny and their two kids. Hagen had offered it to me as an "I'm glad you quit your time-sucking job and came home" present. And I wasn't stupid enough not to accept this over-the-top place.

According to my brothers, I technically owned a quarter of their properties. The fact I had nothing to do with building the empire they'd created didn't seem to faze them. I was their baby sister whether I carried the Lykaios name or not.

I wondered what the crew was going to say when they learned I wasn't planning on living in the penthouse long term. I had my eye on a place close to Henna and Zack's house in the desert. There I saw building a home. But then again, nothing would feel like home until Adrian...

I turned to see my very pregnant sister Henna Lykaios make her way toward me without missing a step in four-inch heels. She had a scowl on her beautiful face that said I was in deep shit.

"I knew you were going to be a no-show for dinner."

Oh shit, I forgot again. Henna had threatened to drag me out of the apartment if I didn't meet her and the girls, meaning Penny and my brother Pierce's wife, Amelia, for dinner. They wanted a girls' night out and I'd bailed on them for the last three times.

"Want to tell me what's going on or do I need to call in backup? I kept Penny and Amelia from storming in here with me. So, I suggest you start talking."

This was Henna's version of a warning that my sisters-in-law were on their way up to make me talk. I was totally about to get ganged up on.

Henna moved to a nearby patio chair and plopped down, kicking off her shoes and setting her feet on an ottoman.

"If Zack saw you wearing those, he would completely lose his shit. Aren't you like fifty months pregnant?"

"Eight. And Zack isn't going to see me, since he's at home with four kids under five and no help since our nanny is sick." There was an almost devilish glint in her eyes. "Well, I guess he does have help. Collin is over for dinner. But those two spend so much time arguing about the right way to cut carrots so the baby doesn't choke that they don't realize the other three are running around naked in the front yard."

Even though Collin was my brothers' biological father, he was my father too, albeit more of a surrogate one. He'd made huge mistakes with his boys, but he'd given Henna and me the type of fatherly love a girl could only dream of. And now he was being the grandfather every kid deserved to have. Although, my family liked to complain he spoiled all the boys with whatever they wanted.

"I never thought my all-business sister and brother-in-law were going to singlehandedly try to populate the earth with the next generation." I shook my head. "I think you've spent the entirety of your marriage pregnant."

"The others were planned. This one—" she pointed to her belly, "—is what happens when one forgets to get her birth control shot in a timely manner and then goes on vacation without kids for the first time in years."

I bit my lip and shifted my attention back to the night.

"Ana. Tell me what's going on?" Henna's voice was filled with worry. "I swear I won't say anything to the guys."

By "guys" she meant my brothers Hagen, Pierce, and Zack.

"There's nothing to tell. I'm ready to be home. At least for the foreseeable future. Plus, I have this kickass job where I get to pretend to be you all day and make people cry."

The minute I'd come home I'd taken over Lykaios International, the casino conglomerate Henna inherited from Collin Lykaios. Henna was ready to pass the torch to me, and I was ready to put the past behind me.

Thankfully I rocked at my job and just negotiated a land deal where we'd build a new casino that would completely put my brothers' casino resorts to shame.

"Tell us what's going on, Anaya," I heard Penny say as she walked onto the deck with Amelia close behind her. "This blowing-us-off shit is getting old."

They both slid into chairs next to Henna and folded their arms as if waiting on a petulant child to talk.

Were these women ever going to see me as more than a

kid sister? I knew they loved me, but I wasn't a child anymore. Hell, I'd done things that would make their heads spin.

"Does the concept of calling before using a private code to access a private penthouse elude you?"

Penny shrugged her shoulders. "You should have changed the code if you didn't want anyone to use it. Now sit your ass down and start talking."

"Like that would have stopped you. Your husband owns the damn building." I huffed and took a seat in the giant round papasan chair in front of the sister squad. "Get it off your chests."

These women had no clue what the issue was but were going to give me a lecture as if they knew all my secrets.

I picked up my water and took a sip.

Henna leaned forward, setting a hand on her belly. "How long have you worked for Solon?"

My eyes widened and I all but choked on the water. "Say that again."

"You heard her." Penny set a hand on her hip. "With Briana as your boss, did you really think I didn't know who you worked for? The crazy woman has been moonlighting as my security for over ten years."

"I have no idea what you're talking about. Bri is not my boss." I set the glass on the table, refusing to look Henna in the eyes.

Henna had this crazy way of knowing when I lied.

Well, technically, Bri was my handler, not my boss. Tara Zain Kumar was the woman in charge.

It was Amelia's turn to add in her two cents. "Ana, did something go wrong?"

The soothing tone of the toughest one of all the women nearly had me cracking.

Amelia was a former Olympic gold medalist in taekwondo and owned one of the largest sports promotion companies in the world. To this day, she trained like she was entering a competition.

"It's complicated."

Amelia reached over, taking my hand in hers. "Did someone break your heart?"

Well, shit. I was going to have to give them something or they'd keep throwing things at me.

Taking a deep breath, I said, "I'm the one who did the leaving."

"He had to have deserved it," Penny interjected. "If he treated you bad, then I say let's find him and kick his ass."

If she only knew that she was talking about her brother, but I loved how loyal she was to me.

"No, he's someone all of you would love." Actually, did love.

Henna studied me. "Then what's the problem? Something happened with him that made you quit a job you loved."

"It's..."

"Complicated," the three women said in unison.

We all grew quiet and then Penny muttered out loud, "I knew it. I fucking knew it."

We all stared at her as if she'd lost her mind.

"Umm, what did you know? And about who?" I asked, seeing the scary gleam in her eyes that she only got when she'd figured out a way to make a better batch of whiskey.

"About you, that explains so much. I am so going to kick Hagen's ass when I get home. This is the reason for the blowup before my wedding."

Amelia frowned. "Penny, are you pregnant or something? You only act this insane when you're knocked up."

"Hey I take offense to that." Henna rubbed her belly.

"How did none of us see it?" Penny stood. "It's Adrian."

I closed my eyes. Fuck. She really was some crazy evil genius.

"What's Adrian?" Henna asked.

"The man she left, the man who's had her all twisted since she started at UNLV. Oh my God, this is fabulous. My baby brother the CIA guy and a Solon agent who probably breaks all the rules."

"Stop. Are you saying my baby sis and your brother are..." Henna stared at me. "OMG that fight the two of you had at Penny's wedding. Don't you remember?"

Oh, I remembered, my husband had told me that

morning he wanted an annulment, my mom finally revealed that she wasn't my biological mother, and I learned my half sister was sleeping with my half brother.

I remained quiet, letting the women discuss me as if I weren't here.

Had Penny just said something about a blowup between Hagen and Adrian?

"Penny," I interrupted, "I need you to rewind and explain what you meant by blowup before your wedding."

All the chatter stopped as Penny sighed.

"The day before my wedding, something happened between Adrian and Hagen—well, actually Pierce and Zack too. Whatever it was, Adrian left a few days later and didn't come home for nearly a year."

And that was when I'd left too. I'd taken all my credits to graduate college early and decided I'd rather be on assignment than walk for graduation.

Dear God, had they forced Adrian to leave me? What could they have used?

I clenched my jaw. "The three of you are going to be widows if I get my hands on them."

My brothers had no idea I could knock each of their overgrown asses out. Size made no difference if you knew exactly where to hit.

Adrian and Sebastian could account for my abilities.

"Oh, the plot thickens." Amelia rubbed her hands together. "So, it's true. You and Adrian?"

I ignored the question and pressed my fingers to the bridge of my nose.

All these years, I was so angry, so confused. One day he was head-over-heels in love with me and the next he was breaking up with me.

I knew my brothers. They had to have used some serious manipulation to get Adrian to back away from me.

The glass in my hand shook, and before I realized what was happening it cracked.

"Woo lady, that's some grip." Amelia plucked the glass from my hand. "I could have used you in the MMA ring."

"Like Pierce would let you."

"Pierce doesn't get to *let* me do anything. These Lykaios men think they're in charge with all their chest-thumping, but they know we'd punch them in the face if they overstepped their bounds."

"Do me a favor, keep my brothers away from me. At least until I'm not so angry with them. Because their inability to see I'm an adult and the fact they can't make up for what our parents did to us are the reasons I've barely come home in the past five years."

"What exactly did they do? Give us something, Anaya." Henna gave me her "I'll beat them up for you" look.

"Promise you guys won't freak?"

"We promise," Penny answered for everyone.

"Adrian and I had been seeing each other since my

freshman year at UNLV. We connected in a way I never expected. He got me. Especially all the crap that came with having a criminal for a father."

I saw Henna flinch. To this day she hadn't gotten over the things she'd gone through because of our father Victor Anthony's embezzlement scandal.

"We fell in love but kept our relationship quiet. You have to admit our family ties are a twisted fucked-up mess."

"I can attest to that. I'm married to my half sister's half brother." Henna rubbed her belly.

"Then I got my internship and both of us knew we were on a time crunch. A week before Penny and Hagen's wedding, we eloped."

"You what?" Henna shouted.

"We aren't married," I added before she went into labor. "A few days later he asked for an annulment. He said we had to go our separate ways. We had to live our dreams and they weren't together."

The pain of the past burned into my chest.

"That explains why you would go out of your way to avoid him. Ana, why didn't you say something? Why didn't you let me be there for you?" Henna's eyes filled with tears. "I'm your sister."

I reached over, squeezing her hand. "Because I wouldn't have let anyone comfort me. I was so hurt and angry. And everyone reminded me of what I'd lost."

"So, you moved to Switzerland to escape."

"Umm, well, I technically don't live there. I am US-based. I have a condo in DC that I share with two other people when I'm not on assignment, but most of the time I hang out in my old condo at the Cypress."

Over the years, I'd mastered sneaking in and out of my condo without anyone knowing I was there. I was usually too tired to go anywhere, and vegging in my own bed was the perfect way to recover.

"Are you saying you've been stealing into your condo for the past few years and we didn't know it?" Henna's voice took on a high pitch. "That you could have been here for numerous events and milestones? Like the birth of your nephews?"

I grimaced. Yeah, those weren't my best moments.

"Calm down, preggers." Amelia pushed Henna back into her chair when she tried to get up.

I threaded my fingers with Henna's. "I'm sorry. I didn't realize how wrong I was to stay away until recently."

"If you aren't here when this baby girl comes, I swear I will kick your ass into the next century."

Henna was everything I'd wanted to be when I grew up. She protected me, dealt with the world for me, made a success of herself so our mother and I could have a future. Seeing how I hurt her made me realize how selfish I'd been to miss so much of her life.

"I promise, I'm not going anywhere. I can't, anyway."

"What does that mean?" Amelia asked.

"Things happened. I can't give you details. Just know I'm not going back."

"What about Adrian?" Penny stared at me.

"What about him?"

The three women glared at me.

At that moment, my phone beeped. Thank God for small favors.

Picking it up, I read the incoming text. Immediately, my heartbeat jumped.

You know the place. I'll come find you.

I stood up, trying to push down the butterflies in my stomach. "I have to go. I'm sorry, but I have to go."

"Where are you going? We aren't done here." Amelia looked as if she was physically going to stop me.

Backing away slowly toward the terrace doors, I said, "I'm sorry. I promise to clear things up later."

Penny shifted her head to the side, studying me. "Are you seriously ditching us?"

"Yep."

"Anaya, what the fuck aren't you telling us?" Henna's temper began to rise again.

"I wouldn't go if this wasn't important. Meet me back here tomorrow morning. I promise it will all make sense." I turned, ready to lock the women on the terrace if they thought to move toward me.

Penny set a palm on Henna's shoulder, stopping her words. "Tell him our kids miss their uncle."

I smiled over my shoulder. "I will."

CHAPTER TWENTY

Adrian

Around midnight, I stepped out onto the private viewing deck on the second story of Vasilissa, one of the Lykaios brothers' most popular clubs. I'd designed every aspect of the security and technical infrastructure of this place. The staff viewed me with the same respect they gave the brothers but without the fear. I spent all my time with them in the back side of the operations, making me one of them as well.

That was why I knew unless I wanted the brothers to know I was here no one would tell them.

Tonight, I was here for my woman.

I moved to a corner in the shadows, giving me a direct view of the dance floor without revealing myself.

Immediately, I spotted her. My Anaya Anthony. My woman.

She was dancing with a group of women. I wasn't sure if they were her friends or people she'd met in the last hour. I should have known she wouldn't follow instructions and wait for me up here.

Not seeing her for the last two months was torture. But it was the only way to make it so no ties to any of my assignments came back to bite me. I knew she'd spent time doing the same thing, especially after the way the Solon team whisked her away. Briana and Jacob had stayed behind, to finish our tasks and give me some story about how it was a ritual to extract an agent like that, but that was total bullshit and a waste of money.

Now we had one more hurdle to overcome to be together.

Her family, my family, our family.

Her hands were thrown in the air as her glorious ass rolled side to side with the rhythm of the Latin beat.

God, was there a more beautiful woman?

The last time I'd been in this club with Ana was five years ago, the weekend of Penny's bachelorette party, the weekend before we'd eloped. Now here we were again, but this time I would ask her and marry her the right way. Not secretly in some chapel no one knew about, but a wedding with our family surrounding us.

Ana threw her head back and laughed as she listened to something one of the women around her said.

I wanted so desperately to go down there and take her into my arms. Or throw her over my shoulder and take her straight out of the club and to my bed.

The crowd shifted and I got the first good look at her dress, if that was what it was. The slightest wrong move and her goods would be on display. Those long legs were for me, not the assholes eye-fucking her from the periphery.

I clenched my teeth. I planned to destroy that thing and paddle her ass for going out in public like this.

As if hearing my irritated thoughts, she looked up in my direction and stopped dancing.

Her eyes grew soft and glazed with tears. Without saying a word to her group, she moved in my direction. She weaved her way through the mass of gyrating bodies, oblivious to anything but me. I turned toward the hallway she was about to come up.

As soon as she came into view, she threw herself into my arms and kissed me. Her heat, her taste exploded in my mouth. She was my heaven.

"God, I missed you, Ana. We're never going to be apart again."

"Ian." She wrapped her legs around my waist and I gripped her ass.

The thong she wore was the only thing separating my

hands from her pussy. I turned us so her back was to a wall and none of the security cameras would get a shot of her ass.

Even if they had, I'd remotely wipe them clean before the night was out.

"Anaya. What the fuck are you wearing?"

She pulled her body back to look at me. "A dress."

"It's indecent."

"And?" She pressed her heels into my ass, grinding her pussy against my jeans-covered cock.

Between kisses, I said, "I am the only man who gets to see your cunt."

"I won't argue with that." Her fingers threaded into my hair. "Take me to that office of yours and fuck me on that petrified-wood desk that shines like high-gloss marble."

I pulled back. "How do you know about the desk?"

It had taken five men to carry the piece into my office.

A wicked smile touched her lips. "I snoop. That's my job. Well, that *was* my job. Even if I wasn't here, there were times I was here."

"You do realize that statement only makes sense to me?"

"That's why we're perfect for each other."

I carried her to a far wall, released my hold on one hip long enough to scan my hand on the fingerprint reader, and then walked through the movable wall.

"One day you're going to tell me how you broke through my security to check out my office."

"One day."

We entered my office and I moved directly to my desk, setting Ana on top.

I stepped back and took in the perfection of the woman who made the ten-thousand-dollar desk look cheap.

"Spread your legs, Ana."

She complied without any hesitation, exposing her soaked underwear.

I grabbed hold of the back of my shirt, pulling it over my head, and threw it on a nearby sofa. Then I opened my pants and freed my cock. I pumped from base to tip, letting precum drip from the slit.

Ana licked her lips.

"Want a taste, baby?"

She nodded, cupping her breasts through her dress and shifting her hips as her pussy grew slicker with need.

I moved in closer, collected my arousal on my fingers, and brought it to her lips. Her mouth wrapped around my fingers and sucked. A moan came from deep in her and my cock jumped.

I grabbed her hips, pulling her to the edge of the desk.

Her arms came around my shoulders. "Fuck me now, Adrian Phillip Kipos. Go slow later."

I paused, realizing this was the first time she'd said my real name, my full name, to me in five years.

"Say that again." I ripped her thong and positioned my cock. "Say my name."

Her arms tightened as she stared into my eyes. "Fuck me, Adrian Phillip Kipos."

I slammed to the hilt inside her soaked pussy.

"Again."

I pulled out and thrust back in.

Her nails dug into my shoulders. "Fuck me, Adrian Phillip Kipos."

"Again," I repeated over and over as I began a relentless pace, pumping hard and fast.

Her pussy walls quickened and her words morphed into, "I love you, Adrian, fuck me harder."

We both exploded in a hot rush of heat, need, and passion.

"What the hell is this?" Hagen Lykaios smacked a paper on the table in front of me.

When I'd slipped out of bed this morning, my only thought was to grab some pastries from the bakery Ana loved and serve her breakfast in bed.

I'd barely made it into the main casino area of the Ida when four overgrown apes stopped me and said my presence was requested by "Mr. Lykaios" at his office in the business tower of the property.

The way it happened was straight-up TV-mafia shit. Either Hagen had been watching too much television or I'd just gotten jaded by the shit I'd dealt with for the past few years.

"If you move your hand then I can tell you."

"You are still fucking married."

I frowned. That couldn't be possible. "I signed the papers."

"Well, according to this, one of you didn't."

I pulled the documents toward me and couldn't hide the grin on my face.

"What the fuck are you smiling at?"

I lifted my gaze to Hagen's. "I planned on marrying her again, so this just saves me the trouble."

"You what?"

"You heard me." I held his gaze. "I fucked up by letting you and your brothers get into my head. She was it for me five years ago and she's it for me now."

"I won't have it. She needs someone stable, someone who won't end up dead, if something went wrong on the job."

"Listen very clearly, Hagen. Just because you're married to my sister doesn't mean you get to tell me how to run my life." I leaned forward. "Do you think I wanted my sister involved with a man who was a fucking mob enforcer? I love her and respect her decisions. You need to do the same for us."

"Ana doesn't even know who you are."

"She knows me better than anyone else."

"Bullshit. Does she know you're CIA or that you've fucked women for the job?"

"As a matter of fact, she does." Hagen and I froze as Ana walked in. "I happened to be his last job."

CHAPTER TWENTY-ONE

Anaya

"She was what?" Hagen shouted.

Adrian closed his eyes and shook his head. "Ana, you aren't helping."

Yeah, I probably shouldn't have phrased my words so bluntly with my over-the-top, powder-keg-tempered brother.

"I'm fucking going to kill you." Hagen reached across the table and grabbed Adrian's collar.

Before I realized I was moving, I grabbed Hagen's arm and flipped him on his back, pressing my boot heel to his throat.

Security rushed in, hearing the commotion, as did Pierce and Zack.

"What the hell, Anaya?" Hagen roared.

Adrian jumped over the table, grabbing me in his arms and moving me across the room.

"Umm. The question is what did you do to piss her off?" Zack walked over to smirk down at Hagen, who only glared at him and then took the hand Zack offered him.

"She was his target. His job. Isn't that how you put it, Anaya?" Hagen's voice was still filled with anger.

"Do you honestly believe she was just a target to me?" Adrian set me on the floor, keeping a hand around my wrist. "Ana, do me a favor. Don't try to save me from them. Hagen is likely to pull out that gun he keeps in the bottom drawer of his desk and shoot me."

"It's not loaded," was my response. "I removed the bullets the last time I was home."

"Why would you do that?" The scowl on Hagen's face was almost comical.

"Because Galen and Markos play in this office and I don't want them to get hurt. Everyone knows they're the nosiest of all the boys."

Pierce noticed the way Adrian angled me behind him. "So, you two are back together?"

"Yes," Adrian and I said together.

"I won't have it," Hagen said.

I moved around Adrian, but he grabbed me, pulling me back. "Let me make this clear so it gets through to your thick skull, and that includes Pierce and Zack too. I am an adult. I don't need your permission. You can't pull the big-brother act on someone who isn't a child."

"And if he's killed on one of his adventures?"

"I know for a fact that won't happen," I said.

This time Pierce spoke while folding his giant arms across his chest. "Explain to us how."

"Because he's out."

Zack stepped in front of Adrian and me, staring me straight in the eyes. "And what about you? Are you out? Am I going to be able to sleep at night without worrying that you're dead somewhere?"

Of course, he would know, if Henna knew. But from the shock on my other two brothers' faces, Penny and Amelia had kept that tidbit of information from them.

"Same. No more international assignments or staying away from home."

A slow smile broke out on my handsome brother's face and Zack stepped around Adrian to kiss my forehead.

My eyes clouded. When was the last time any of my brothers showed me affection other than lecturing me?

I pushed past Adrian and wrapped my arms around Zack. "I love you too."

After a few moments, I pulled back.

"Can someone please explain what the hell is going on? I am lost. And why isn't anyone pissed off that they are still married after we told the asshole to end it." Hagen's blue eyes were filled with a mix of confusion and irritation.

I couldn't help but laugh.

Then I realized what he'd said. *Still married? Told the asshole to end it?*

I lifted my hand. "Pause and rewind. You made Ian ask for an annulment?"

Everyone remained quiet. My temper flared and I counted backward from ten so I wouldn't punch one of the many moronic men in the room.

Finally, Pierce spoke. "You were twenty-one with a life ahead of you. You deserved to pursue your dreams and not get stuck here waiting for someone who could end up dead if any of his assignments went south. Plus, he wasn't much older than you."

I closed my eyes and pressed my fingers to my temples. "So, what I'm hearing you say is that you took the decisions for my life out of my hands just like everyone else has done since I was born."

"We were protecting you. We didn't want you to regret things in the future." Hagen came around his desk.

"Like when my biological mother gave me to another woman to raise as her child? Or when Collin, Mom, and Henna kept the truth of my birth a secret from me? I've spent so much of my life wondering who I was because of these decisions. And now I learn you kept the only man I've ever loved from me for my own good. It's just too much." My voice cracked. "Do you know why I left home? I couldn't handle the memories, the pain of knowing I wasn't wanted, the pain of what my father did to all of us. And you know what brought me back? Him." I pointed to Adrian.

"Because I was so focused on succeeding at my work and forgetting my past, I made mistakes and got caught. He risked his life to get me back. He gave up his career to be with me. I won't let anyone or anything take him from me again."

I moved, ready to storm out of Hagen's office, but Adrian slipped an arm around my waist and turned me toward his chest. "Ana, I'm to blame too. I let my insecurities win out. Your brothers love you. They wanted to give you what they felt like they never had. A future outside of Vegas."

I lifted my face and scanned my brothers' expressions. Each looked devastated.

"Anaya, I'm sorry," Hagen whispered, dropping his head. "You are the last piece of Mama that we have and we went overboard trying to keep you with us. In the end, it pushed you away."

That was another thing that was so hard to deal with—they always saw the mother they'd lost to cancer, a mother who loved them so much, the mother who had an affair and had a baby with another man, a mother who didn't love me enough to keep me.

"God, can you forgive us?" Zack asked.

"Do the girls know the details?"

Pierce winced and shook his head.

"If you want my forgiveness, each of you need to face your wives and tell them what you did."

"I'd rather walk over hot coals," Hagen grumbled with Pierce and Zack agreeing.

Hagen then said, "You have a deal."

I gave them a weary smile. "Now can I be alone with my husband?" I made sure to emphasize the "husband" part.

"You're kicking me out of my own office?" Hagen gave me an incredulous look.

"Yep."

"If you're a brat as a twenty-six-year-old, I shudder to think what you were like as a kid to poor Henna," Zack added, moving to the door.

Pierce followed Zack, with Hagen being the last.

The door was left open as if Hagen was worried Adrian and I would jump each other. It wouldn't surprise me if Hagen was just outside, listening to everything we said.

I waited a few seconds before I spoke. "So we're married. How did that one slip through the cracks?"

Adrian's lips curved up at the corners. "One of us didn't file their signature with the court."

"I'm going to assume you're referring to me."

I thought back to that time and remembered getting the annulment papers and the heartache seeing them caused. But I couldn't recall if I ever signed them. Everything during those days was a haze. At the time, my focus was getting out of Vegas.

"So, we're married."

"We're married," he agreed.

"Thank goodness for small favors."

"How's that?"

"We brought back something from the island." I moved Adrian's hand from my waist to over my stomach. "In our family, marriage is a requirement for this phase of life."

His gaze burned into mine before the seriousness on his face was replaced by a huge grin.

"You're pregnant?"

I nodded as my heart contracted seeing the joy on his face. "We're pregnant."

"You're what?" Hagen roared.

Both Adrian and I couldn't help but laugh. Instead of answering my nosy brother, Adrian threaded his fingers into my hair and kissed me.

"I love you, Anaya Serina Anthony."

"I love you, Adrian Phillip Kipos."

I smiled up, seeing Adrian's heart in his green eyes. "So now what?"

"Not sure. What do two ex-spies do when they get back home?"

"Live like normal people?" I asked, just as some

costumed show performers dressed as lavish human-sized birds walked by the open doors of Hagen's office.

We both laughed.

"In Vegas, that's all relative."

"Then I guess we'll have to figure it out as we go."

"As long as you're with me, I couldn't agree more."

THE END

Turn the page for more detail

**Master of Control (Gods of Vegas – Book 5)
Only Available in the Leave Me Breathless:
Black Rose Collection (Available Now)**

Preorder - www.books2read.com/blackrosecollection

I'm a prize, a treasure, something to cherish. Or so I've been told.
But I know the truth. I'm a commodity recently sold to the highest bidder.
Sebastian Weber is ruthless, heartless, calculating, and my

new husband. Power is the weapon he wields and control is his game.

I should fear him, resent him, but instead I'm drawn to him, craving his slightest touch, wanting every part of him. Leaving him isn't an option, and ***staying means shattering his world.***

GODS OF VEGAS, BOOK 1

Read the first book in the Gods of Vegas Series:

www.books2read.com/masterofsin

He is the right man, for all the wrong things.

It was always him...
The one I shouldn't want, shouldn't crave, the one who could destroy my carefully built life.
Hagen Lykaios was the essence of sin, indulgence, and danger - everything I knew to avoid.
All it took was one unexpected touch, and he consumed me, left me begging, needy, and hungry for more.
He said if I entered his world he would corrupt me, own me, and change all that I had ever known...and you know what? ***I went anyway.***

www.books2read.com/masterofsin

ABOUT THE AUTHOR

Inspired by her years working in corporate America, Sienna loves to serve up stories woven around confident and successful women who know what they want and how to get it, both in – and out – of the bedroom.

Her heroines are fresh, well-educated, and often find love and romance through atypical circumstances. Sienna treats her readers to enticing slices of hot romance infused with empowerment and indulgent satisfaction.

Sienna loves the life of travel and adventure. She plans to visit even the farthest corners of the world and delight in experiencing the variety of cultures along the way. When she isn't writing or traveling, Sienna is working on her "happily ever after" with her husband and children.

Sign up for her newsletter to be notified of releases, book sales, events and so much more.

www.siennasnow.com

BOOKS BY SIENNA SNOW

Rules of Engagement

Rule Breaker

Rule Master

Rule Changer

Politics of Love

Celebrity

Senator

Commander

Gods of Vegas

Master of Sin

Master of Games

Master of Revenge

Master of Secrets

Master of Control

Collections

Take Me To Bed: Bedime Quickies

Intrigued By Love

Reckless Romeo (A Cocky Hero Club Novel) - 2020

Kings of Cyprus

Coming Fall 2020